Mark O'Flynn has published five collections of poems, most recently *The Soup's Song*. His poetry and short fiction have appeared in many Australian journals as well as overseas. His novels include *Grassdogs* and *The Forgotten World*. He has also published the comic memoir *False Start* and a collection of short fiction, *White Light*. He lives in the Blue Mountains.

Also by Mark O'Flynn

Fiction
Captain Cook
Grassdogs
The Forgotten World
White Light (short stories)

Non-Fiction
False Start

Poetry
The Too Bright Sun
The Good Oil
What Can Be Proven
Untested Cures
The Soup's Song

THE
LAST
DAYS
OF AVA
LANGDON

MARK O'FLYNN

First published 2016 by University of Queensland Press
PO Box 6042, St Lucia, Queensland 4067 Australia

www.uqp.com.au
uqp@uqp.uq.edu.au

Cover design by Christabella Designs
Cover image by Anna Pogossova/Getty Images
Typeset in 12.5/17.5 pt Adobe Caslon Pro by Post Pre-press Group, Brisbane
Author photograph by Barbara Fitzgerald
Printed in Australia by McPherson's Printing Group

National Library of Australia
Cataloguing-in-Publication data is available at http://catalogue.nla.gov.au

ISBN
978 0 7022 5415 4 (pbk)
978 0 7022 5778 0 (ePDF)
978 0 7022 5779 7 (ePub)
978 0 7022 5780 3 (Kindle)

University of Queensland Press uses papers that are natural, renewable and
recyclable products made from wood grown in sustainable forests. The logging and
manufacturing processes conform to the environmental regulations of the country
of origin.

In memory of my father
Tim O'Flynn
1926–2015

It is absurd to say that the age of miracles is past. It has not yet begun.

– Oscar Wilde, *Letter from Paris*, 1900

DREAM

SHE IS LOST IN THE FOREST looking for two heart-shaped leaves, but they are terribly hard to find. She fossicks for them everywhere. No one tree has two identical heart-shaped leaves, at least not the ones she has examined. For some reason it is important that she find two the same. The forest rustles in the dark with the sound of the sea. She may be wrong, she may be seeing difference where difference does not exist, but it is the heart-shaped leaves which seem to be the odd ones out; that is, the distortion amongst the norm, perhaps even the mutation. She hopes this is not so, she wouldn't like to think of it being so. She runs from tree to tree. Every one is different, and every leaf of every tree is different also, so why not every cell of every leaf? There are plenty of leaves in the shape of a heart, plenty of the greeting-card and Valentine's Day hearts, but in the natural world she can find no two the same, not even from the same tree. Gum trees appear to have the greatest incidence of this heart-shaped anomaly, some with lumps and bunions. Fuel for the fire. Others torn and made to fit an unfamiliar mould. The greeting-card heart is an idealised shape. It's too perfect. There is no resemblance to the heart's actual function, which is to provide a conduit between the body and the other. Isn't it? To palpitate the ethereal clay. Placed horizontally, bisected with a scalpel, the shape looks more like a whale, some leviathan breaching. Sound of the sea slapping at the green and greasy legs of a pier. The crashing of dishes. A cartoon whale. Two symmetrical halves, sundered. A shape that might be placed together again, belly to belly, to form a whole. Repaired. Scarred. A creature breaking forth from its element into the smoky air.

MORNING

DAWN CRACKS LIKE AN EGG against the fibro walls of the derelict shack. An egg? Is that quite the right assessment? The yolky light makes itself known to the windows. She can smell it. The eastern sky pales quickly through the trees. Within the walls she has already been awake for over an hour listening to the various creatures rustling outside, inside, tramping about, creating bigger footsteps than they own. The blankets pulled up to her chin. The bedsprings squeaking their familiar dirge. There are other noises in the ceiling she doesn't recognise. On the plaster overhead a galaxy of mildew.

And now the light is hatching, she has no excuse. She sits up. Her breath steams into the cold air of the room. A porcelain doll sits watching her from the top of the wardrobe, its hair sticking up in tufts. Miss Min-Mog. *Bonjour.* The curtains are yellow in the windows, cadmium yellow originally, now faded to the colour of jaundice. Again, not quite right, but it will have to do — she hasn't got her thinking cap on yet. One of the cats sits with its nose to the gap between the bedroom wall and the floorboards. That's where the draught and the smell of death get in.

The ash benign in the fireplace. The language of dreams dropping away. Blackened leaves fragile in the grate like the shadows of leaves.

Morning at last.

Her feet search for their slippers under the cot. She locates one. Where's the other? Never mind, she'll find it in a minute. She yawns broadly, her mouth tacky. The cats stir and move about her legs, purring for favour. She goes to the dunny bucket just by the entrance to the bedroom (it'll be freezing outside, there'll be frost), and, sitting, lets the last dregs of the night drain away. She'll empty it later. She stamps her feet to get the circulation back into them. Her liver gives a lurch. She feels it. *Pissupprest*: there's a word, the holding in of urine. She's got to learn to get up in the night more, but what's the point? Funnel-web spiders migrating across the floor give her the willies. She knows they're not after her, per se, but nevertheless they're another worry. Other creatures besides. A slug underfoot in the middle of the night can cast sleep to the wind. Catching sight of herself in a little wedge of mirror perched on an exposed joist, she stops. Who is that hideous creature? What form dost thou take? Her hair like the thatch from a mattress used for nesting material, with lavender bags under her eyes.

It is Ava, she thinks. It is me. If only I had another life.

If only she had another life. If only she could have been born someone else; it's a small enough change. Another woman. A child. Oscar Wilde, for instance. Why not? What might that have been like? To be someone else. Resurrection.

She lies on the kitchen floor – is that her lying there? No blanket pulled up to her chin.

The mildew.

She goes to the kitchen door – the only door – and opens it to the wind. The scrub is still there, close and claustrophobic. If anything, it has come a little closer during the night, as if it is playing Grandma's Footsteps, and has only just frozen motionless now that she is watching. What's the time, Mr Wolf? Their leaves wash in the wind. She's right. On the clear patches of ground near her washing line there is frost. Her singlets hang out there stiff with cold. The morning light is weaving between the trees to the east, birds adamant about the dawn. Frost lies on the outside water tank also. Everything still. At her feet upon the welcoming stone is spread a tiny explosion of feathers. Which one of them has done this? she asks herself, giving the nearest cat behind her a toe-poke out the door.

'Bastards,' she curses, and slams it shut. The house shudders. The other cats all seem to have vamoosed. They know when to stay out of her way. Ava on the warpath. Hurricane Ava. The sudden tempest of her anger in the air. Perhaps they have gone for good?

She stirs the ash in the grate with a twig. The scorched leaves disintegrate. An old plough disc sits at the back of the hearth like a Chinese soldier's breastplate. She finds a warm coal at the fire's core. It glows with exposure to the air. She piles on some newspaper and kindling kept in a box for just this purpose. The headline in the paper says *Junie Morosi love nest*, but that is of no concern to Ava. Good luck to her. That is not why she has the paper. It's a few weeks old anyway. She puffs and pants at the grate, blowing up gusts of ash until the paper catches. The exertion makes her dizzy, which is okay. Ava does not dislike dizziness as a state of being in the world, she tells herself, trying to ratify her thoughts into a state of kitchen-sink sagacity. She does not discriminate between one point of view and another. Male, female, you, me, alive, dead. The world would sometimes seem to demand it, an altered state of dizziness, or so she thinks, and what a time of day to be thinking it. Why did she get up so early? Apart from her usual night terrors. The slugs underfoot. Ah yes, she remembers, the appointed time is nigh. She needs to prepare.

Against the wall, on the kitchen table – the only table – under a stone paperweight lies the wrapped parcel containing *The Saunteress*. The typewriter beside it with its mouth closed. *Imperial Model T Made in Leicester, England.* Oh the sparks it spat out yesterday, she recalls, those keys falling like slain infantrymen on the fields of Flanders, resurrected, marching on. Today will be a great day. She circles the date on the calendar and scrawls *Great day* beside it. On the calendar is a picture of a ghost gum in snow. The first of June, 1974. No other date is circled for this month. Nor the one previous, but she's not going to revisit that. Time past is time past, but what glories time continuing contains. Soon the fire is blazing away and all the last vestiges of her dreams have been banished. Is that too strong a phrase for it? Banishment. Exile. Never mind. Let all the creatures that lurk in the shadows begone. She stomps about the house making a ruckus, claiming back the definition of the walls, her space within them. And also to give the spiders something to think about if they want to mess with her. And the warmth. She opens the door – the only door – glances out, slams it again. I am here. Beyond the windows the bush seems to have taken a step backwards and the faces hidden in the mistletoe look away. A bird whistles nearby. There's no denying it. Time for breakfast.

The Weeties sit in the high cupboard. The rats do not appear to have disturbed them. But the packet is nearly empty and here's the first dilemma of the day. She can be frugal and divide what's left so as to stretch her resources. A small, miserly breakfast today, another one tomorrow, averting starvation like a gastropod crawling along on her stomach over the mossy ground. Or she can splurge and enjoy a good old satisfying banquet now, and hang tomorrow. Who likes moss, anyhow? Cross that bridge when the river rises. Luck is with her. It is, after all, a great day. Why? Because of the parcel on the table. Because of its imminent voyage and all that is invested in it.

The milk bottle is outside in a bucket with a square sheet of tin on top and a rock weighing it all down to stop the crows having a go. A clever bird is the crow, its feathers as black as snow. No, that's not right. Like describing the light as 'yolky', that's just an affected prose style. Kitchen-sink foolishness. Outside it's the coldest place. The milk might even be frozen. She goes to check. It's not. She has all the Weeties. May as well be hung for a sheep as a lamb, Ava decides. While she eats, a rat pokes its pink nose out of the hidey-hole and twitches at the air. She's careful not to startle it. From the wall it approaches tentatively along the table, yet

11

with gumption enough. Brave little fellow, really. Ava takes a single Weetie flake from the bowl and delicately holds it between thumb and fingertip. It is shaped like a tiny comet. She stretches her arm out along the Formica table-top, slowly, subsiding gently, until they meet in the middle near the type-writer. She lies awkwardly like that for a time. The rat sniffs, then takes the flake of cereal between his paws. He holds it like a supplicant with a holy chalice and nibbles. Which one is he? Plutus or Bacchus? Ah yes, Bacchus, she can tell by the mottled, albinotic pink near the base of his tail. She has to sit up and the sudden movement makes the rat scurry off through its alcove into the wall cavity, presumably to share its news. Is this reading too much into it? Yolky light, what was she thinking? And a gastropod? More things in Heaven and earth, Red.

Ava eats. She shovels in the Weeties like they're going out of fashion. She tips up the bowl to her mouth and slurps down the last of the milk. Her stomach sings happily. Afterwards she takes a butter knife and carefully slits the empty cardboard box along each edge so that, after the operation, she is left with two perfect matching rectangles. She places King Willy Weeties face down on her stockpile on top of the cupboard for later. She stares at the grey sheets. The blank canvas of her day ahead.

Cardboard scraps in the fire – *whoosh* – breakfast bowl in the sink – *clatter*.

The day ahead.

On the windowsill her dolls sit side by side watching the room. Other dolls sit on the bookshelf: one in between

12

Immanuel Kant and Enid Blyton, another separating *The Magic Pudding* and Aristophanes. Not to mention the works of Ava Langdon. Two books. Or rather ten copies each of two books, which makes it look so much more impressive. *The Apple Pickers*, yellowing now, in pride of place, and beside it *The Golden Cravat*. Her oeuvre. And, of course, the immortal medal.

She untucks her singlet, holds it to her nose and inhales. It's a bit ripe. Not quite the clobber for such an auspicious occasion as today. She dashes outside to the line. Her feet scuff the leaves and twigs. Look, she's managed to find the other slipper. Where did that come from? She unpegs a clean singlet and scampers back to the warmth, the relative warmth, of the hut. She holds the singlet in front of the hearth to thaw it out, flaps the ghosts of frost from it. She whips off the old one. It has ink stains on it. She rolls it in a ball and tosses it into a corner. From her skin she unpeels the sheets of newspaper that have lined her singlet through the night. Some of them stick to her. These she tosses onto the fire. They roar up the chimney like flaming parrots. There's a smudge of newsprint on her belly, but who is going to see that? She sluices some cold water from the tap into her armpits and rubs vigorously. Christ that's cold. The dolls think so. She thinks so. It's the middle of winter. She pulls on the clean singlet, which is toasty warm now and gives definition to her biceps. Next, off with the pyjama bottoms and on with the big white underpants. What did that awful boy call them? She hobbles from foot to foot like a flamingo on hot coals. Don't trip over, old girl, she says to herself, you might do yourself an injury, you might freeze to the floor and stick, like a dog's tongue to a block of ice.

Next: inside the wardrobe she reveals the pinstriped trousers hanging neatly folded from a coat hanger. She brushes them down with the flat of her hand and lays them on the cot. They are beautiful, the cut of the cloth and the line of them. Oscar Wilde would take Piccadilly by storm in trousers like those. She places a cream linen shirt above the trousers, and if she squints, blurring her eyes, yes, they match, forming the simulacrum of a man. A man on her bed, albeit a flattened, two-dimensional man. Hello, stranger. The opal cufflinks? The bowtie? No, a cravat for today. The gorgeous yellow one. She takes it from her chest of drawers (a slice of cardboard under one foot to stop it rocking). She pulls on the trousers and clips the braces to the waistband. The elastic snaps at her shoulder. She loves that sound, crisp as a rifle shot on a winter's morning. Last of all, the overcoat, like a plundered bear, or a Cossack's embrace. She wraps it around herself like a chieftain. All these similes. She could weather blizzards in this coat, climb glaciers. She could metamorphose. Ava contemplates whiskers, but a glance out the window to the north, plus the feeling in her kidneys, tells her it may well rain today. It's not beyond the realm of possibility. And a sagging, waterlogged beard would be unbecoming, in Piccadilly as it is in Katoomba; it would not serve the purpose it was designed for. God's design. Or at least some immortal fellow. But what purpose? The glory of Man? Hardly. It's still too early in the morning for this sort of plum-pudding rhetoric. She belches voluptuously. Or rather, eructates, if you prefer – she can after all be a lady. Her heart gives a hop, skip and a jump in relief. Ah, so far life is pretty good. Now, what about shoes? The choice is limited. These plastic sandals? Or the thongs? No, too cold. Her chilblains. How about these staunch campaigners (she selects the steel-capped work boots), conquerors of abstract lands. Boots of yore. Head kickers.

As she buttons up the linen shirt a transformation takes place. Her spine straightens, shoulders pushed back. She strikes a pose in the mirror. The line of her jaw appears more chiselled, carved from granite, as if she was daring someone to knock her down, to challenge her to a duel with a white glove. Gloves? No, not today. She knots the cravat expertly at her throat. What a figure she shall make. Cut? Caper? Confabulate? What an imago, an illiquation. Inside her head and outside of it. The two rats, Plutus and Bacchus, emerge from their crevice, ostensibly in search of more Weeties, but also to inspect the ritual, the opening gambit of her getting ready for the day. She twirls for them. No, twirling is the wrong verb for the wrong gender. Instead she *promenades* (although there is the tiny residue of a girl in her that enjoys the sensation of the twirl).

'What do you think, lads?'

She brushes her hair. She rubs a pomade of perfumed hair gel into it and smooths it flat. God's grease. She takes a breath. And she is done. *Voilà.*

Voilà. Yes. In a flash of doubt she opens the not-yet-sealed parcel on the table and gently removes the contents, *The Saunteress*. She feeds the last page of the typescript into the roller of the typewriter, lovely sound of the ratchets. It's a sound

15

that sends shivers rippling across her scalp, like a peacock's tail over a corrugated roof. She rolls it up and down until she finds the spot, a gap between the penultimate paragraph and the – what's the word? – the antepenultimate one. The one before that. Just the spot. She flexes her fingers and types:

> He raised his chiselled chin as if he was daring someone to knock him down and challenge him to a duel with a white glove.

Perfect. Slightly longer than the space available, but no matter, all her life has been the pursuit of the perfect line. The line of her jaw, the line of her pinstriped trousers, the line to encapsulate a God she doesn't necessarily believe in but would like to capture anyway. She whips, no, not whips, carefully releases the captured page from the roller and returns it to its place in the rose-coloured pile. *Consummatum est.* She picks up the cover letter placed atop the title page and reads it once again.

> To the Senior Editor
> Angus & Robertson
>
> Dear Senior Editor,
>
> Please find enclosed my latest manuscript, the first option on which I offer to you exclusively. I think you will find this is my best work yet. And after all I have put into it how could it not? It will finally bring to a conclusion the trilogy – may

I say the prize-winning trilogy – we have achieved together. To think it has been over twenty years since we last conspired in Art's great adventure.

If your decision is to accept this manuscript for publication then would you please reply to Ava Langdon, care of Katoomba Post Office, at your earliest convenience? If, however, your decision is the converse then could I ask you to address your correspondence to Mr Oscar Wilde, care of the same address, above.

Oscar can handle the rejection.

Alas, I cannot.

If this latter is the case then I would beseech you to preserve the manuscript for me in the bowels of your deepest archive, don't fret about publishing, merely guard it with all your being. I shall be o'erlooking from the vaults of Heav'n.

Yours in sincere anticipation

Ava Langdon.

Ava compares the tone of this to her last cover letter, or was it the one before? Where she declared – what were her words again? Yes, that they were reducing her to *a puking, retching gangrenous corpse*. That had some style: *a puking, retching gangrenous corpse*. This is much more civil and optimistic. She slips the two rubber bands around the whole bundle. She slides the wad of paper, all four hundred pages of it, like a brick, back into its parcel, and places it in her calico bag. Bag, it's more of a sack really, but it's all she has. It has its own memories, its own sense of ambition. She glances at herself in the window's reflection. What's missing? Ah, the final touch – her white topi, the pith helmet lined in red velvet hanging on its nail beside the photograph of Red with her heart-shaped face. I dips my lid.

She is ready. With her helmet she can face the world.

The rats have disappeared.

Before she leaves, Ava takes another sheet of newspaper from the basket by the fire. The headline is something about Mr Whitlam. She's heard of him. Been in the news a bit lately, although she doesn't really care why. She opens the door and, crouching carefully so as not to spoil her trousers, she picks up the bloodied feathers that are lying on the welcoming stone. She lays them side by side on the sheet of paper, the quills all pointing in the same direction, though not the feet, curled in a final clutching spasm; these she tosses aside. She wraps the feathers in the paper, folding it delicately but firmly. Then, locating a square of chicken wire amongst the scraps scattered outside the shack she folds it around the parcel of feathers, bends flat the wire ends so they do not snag. She takes it inside and adds it to the others in a corner by the tubs under a window. A great day. A day with great purpose, looming large.

With helmet on and thoughts focused, Ava picks up her bag of priceless cargo, her coat and machete, and starts her adventure. She locks the flimsy wooden door behind her and pockets the key, even though she knows it wouldn't take much to knock the door down altogether or pull it completely off its hinges. There is just the one door. It is the only way in or out.

The cats follow her as far as the old bus in which she keeps her other, less valuable things. It is the shell of an old school bus, speckled with rust, that she cannot lock. Nothing to write home about. More feathers. Rocks wrapped in chicken wire. Memorabilia. Dried flowers the meaning of which she has forgotten. Never mind. What does a door symbolise? A door, adore. With each step she takes, the world expands before her, opening up like a lotus. She inhales mightily. As the breath in her breast swells, the pain in her organs, the appendix and pancreas specifically, correspondingly recedes. Ava is acutely aware of these quirky hiccups inside her. All except the pain in her heart which has been a lifelong tribulation, like her tricky knee, despite which she marches forth. Forth and forthwith. And don't a machete and a white pith helmet, albeit a faded one, make for marching as the most suitable form of peram-bulation? Yes, they do. She gives the helmet a tap. She needs to get the fluids circulating, find the tide of the day and float with it. Her joints and limbs start to loosen up. It doesn't take long for the blood to start galloping in her like a puppy after a ball.

Birds chatter in the trees as Ava sets out on her expedition. She steps onto Princes Road, which is not very princely. She follows it for a couple of cricket pitches then steps through the trees into the nearby orchard owned by the local madwoman, Swami Apogee, or whatever her crazy name is. Strange that her neighbour should be a madwoman. Ava thinks about that phrase. The grass is crisp with frost. Her old brown boots crunch through it. In summertime there are cherries, and nectarines and peaches. However, today there are only a few left-over walnuts, their shells like wizened brains, some apricots and some unripe figs. Ava picks a few and puts them in her pockets. Swami Apogee, in her skillion-roofed farmhouse, has been supplementing Ava's diet like this for years. In summer it's quite lucrative, perhaps nutritious is the better word. Swami no doubt believes in sharing and would let Ava take whatever she wanted, if only she would ask. She watches Ava roving like a bee from tree to tree in a measured dance. At least Ava imagines Swami watching her. Ava's imagination brings sentience to the world and casts it in a luminous light, like looking at a dragonfly in a bottle. Her hand briefly touches the bark of every tree trunk. For Ava the orchard is a gentle reminder of those glory days when she went fruit picking with Red, the way breakfast is the reminder of every breakfast and is, in fact, an echo of the breast. An orchard is a place of whispering, familiar voices. Where are they now, her happy ghosts? Why, alive in her heart, that's where. How long has the orchard, originally propagated by monks, been here surrounded by bush? Ava does not know, but she offers up a vote of thanks to the old forward-thinking Franciscans who planted it in the first place. Good lads, those chaps. She wonders if she has it in her heart to be a Franciscan. A vow of silence? Hardly. A vow of genius. Yes, more like it.

She eats a few withered apricots. Weeties and apricots, what better way to start the day's great mission? Several parrots and rosellas are helping themselves to the highest fruits that have not fallen. Ava knows all about them, the opportunists who provide a sense of continuity in the harvest; some for the birds, some for the market stall. At her feet in the grass the acrid stink of fermenting apples. She moves on before her neighbour takes it into her head to apprehend her. What a silly name, Swami Apogee. Ava supposes it has some sort of significance, like a dried flower. A commune of some denomination, she believes. People heading in and out, wearing funny clothes. They never stay long. She has seen them come and go, living a life she can only wonder at. Enlightenment, she supposes it is they're after. Well, good luck to them. If only she could glimpse inside their heads, then she would know what was wrong with them, though why would you want to? Murky-grey is the only sense of clarity Ava's ever had, apart from that moment when a book comes alive in her and eclipses everything. Then look out. Perspicacity, oh yes. It's the vision she carries burning in her mind's eye as she returns to the road, her footsteps striding behind her in the frost like something with small feet following. Ava turns to the right and takes the next step.

* * *

It's a fair hike from her hut into town. The demons of the night at last shrugged off. A puddle from yesterday has a crust of ice on it, flawed and fractured, bubbles trapped underneath. She toes it with her boot until it cracks, and moves on.

It's about three or four miles in the old money and it never gets any shorter. Sometimes, purely for variety, she cuts through the scrub to the cemetery by the hospital; it's hardly a shortcut, distracted as she sometimes is by the narrative of the headstones, or the inquisitive pleasure of the grave-digger on his back-hoe excavating a plot. Rabbits dig and make play amongst the stones. It adds a bit more time to the trek, but there's less traffic, and what has she but time? However, that is normally a summertime distraction and it is not summer.

Ava's hut is the furthest building, the furthest anything, from town on the north side of the highway at the end of the dirt track, beyond the last of the bitumen. Beyond her hut Tenth Avenue dwindles off into the scrub. Why she lives out here she sometimes has to struggle to remember. Then the circumstances of her ownership come back in no particular order. She imagines the people, the women in their houses behind the photinias and rhododendrons, as she strolls past, peering at her from behind their lace curtains. What would it be like to be them? The novelist in her is curious. People used to be able to tell the time by Immanuel Kant's daily jaunt to the shops. She wonders if she is of that calibre. An engineer in the machine that maketh the world turn. Smoke rises from their chimneys as if it is the signature of domestic civilisation. What do they see, these women? Resplendent gentleman on his morning constitutional? Intrepid explorer of other worlds – or untamed harpy? She has been called all these things. And worse. She contains multitudes. Immanuel Kant, he sounds like he had a few problems.

In the distance, to the left of Queens Road, in a shallow valley a flock of cockatoos sits in the tree tops like a fistful of desiccated coconut. They rasp and croak to each other in what can only be called communion. Or at least what she can only call communion, though perhaps it is enterprise? A language not of her understanding. For every word there is a better word. She marches on. See Ava marching. Left, right, left, right, hup hup hup. Sometimes, as now, Ava has the sense of inhabiting another body just to the side of herself, a couple of picture frames back in the movie, from where she is able to watch herself, see herself from the outside being brilliant. Sometimes, after a hard night, Ava shuffles on her old bones, yet today in her mind she is striding out. *Good morning to you ladies*, she says to herself, even going so far as to tip her hat. Her helmet. Ava tipping her helmet. A sola topi of the classic style worn in the wilds of the old Limpopo, all set about with eucalyptus trees. It's her Rudyard Kipling hat. One of her prized possessions, dispensing one thought at a time like a copper coin to the beggar boys. A little the worse for wear now, with the passage of time, the shade of old lemons, but proud (if hats can have pride) of its battle wounds. Tooth mark, claw mark, bullet ricochet. Faded saffron urinous yellow, but that is hardly the topi's fault. To grow old. Age has its virtues. People notice her in this helmet. It's her tiger-shooting helmet. She strikes a commanding pose, just for a second. Wonderful word, *eucalyptus*.

'Garn, you old nut case.'

A voice. A boy's voice. A beggar boy, yelling out at her from the verandah of his house. She stops. He is holding a stick. Perhaps he has been pretending it is a gun. Here is an example, the first of the day, of what she might term recalcitrant youth. No respect for their elders. How would you go about *understanding* them? She is not envious of the young, but that does not mean she has to like them.

'I remember you, my boy,' she calls.

The boy framed by the pale cladding of the house. She remembers his luminous red hair, the freckles like semi-colons all over his face, the gangly limbs seemingly with lives of their own. A magpie would like a lock of that hair for her nest.

When she stops, her words make the boy drop his stick and scoot around the corner of the house and disappear. He runs like a scarecrow on fire. Another voice comes from within:

'Eddie, get in here.'

Ava wonders if she should go up to the house. Enter the yard, climb up the steps and knock on the door. Knock *commandingly* on the door, and interrupt the baking. *Excuse me, madam, but some things are beyond the pale.* She wonders if she should confront the boy. The rudeness of this creature. Should she take the brat out from under the table and bend him over her knee and paddle his backside with the flat of her machete. You see if I wouldn't, she thinks. *Oh my baby*, the mother might cry, or else the mother would be thankful. *There, good lady wife, pray wipe your tears. Your gratitude is thanks enough.* Ava realises she has no idea *what* a mother might think if you took to her child with a machete, irrespective of the moral righteousness of it. Surely as a writer she should have a greater understanding of what goes on in the minds of others. She must try harder. However, this is not the time or place to go about dispensing charity. More pressing matters. Maybe it wasn't her the boy was calling out to? Should she give him the benefit of the doubt? That would be the generous thing to do. A sweet child. Once suckling babe. Yes. Ride on, stranger. She hoists the calico bag higher on her shoulder, lifts her head and rides on. Well, walks in a cloud of indifferent nobility. The white net drapes shift slightly as she passes.

She's puffing like a heifer by the time she gets to the top of the hill near the highway, her pulse dancing a merry old jig. Trucks rumble past, east and west on their way to important assignations. All that cargo. The world is speeding up, though still, for Ava, at walking pace. She passes the hospital, averting her eyes. If she cannot see it, then it does not exist. If it does not exist, then it cannot harm her. Is this what Immanuel Kant has taught? No, someone else. She blocks her ears and hums – *la la la*. Instead she watches a train rattle west towards Lithgow, that bleak star. Nothing wrong with trains.

The helmet not only stops her thoughts from escaping, from leaking out her ears, it also stops other, wayward thoughts from entering at inappropriate moments. She walks. See Ava walking. It never gets any faster, walking pace, but sometimes she barely notices the journey at all. Good ideas come to her while she's walking. Like today, suddenly here she is passing the old Renaissance School with its tall fenestrated tower, and the sandstone courthouse (more trouble brewing), and look – already at the Council Chambers. Bullshit Castle, as she's heard it called. Not yet open for business. What goes on in there is beyond imagining, but she'll give it a go: arcane rites and sacrifice. Goats slaughtered on the mayoral table, Ava wouldn't be surprised, to the tune of bagpipes and smoky incense.

She crosses the highway. A truck honks its Klaxon at her because she has not waited for the green light. She never does.

The passing truck's slipstream buffets her. Ava doesn't abide by petty constraints and regulations. It's a philosophical position. There are enough pedantic rules in this world. She's more of a footpath anarchist. Revolution at ground level. She wonders if her mind will ever slow down to match the pace of her feet; she has to pull her helmet down to her ears.

She passes the first hotel, Gearins, then nips across the railway line, boom gates up like bayonets. Behind her an EH Holden bumps and rattles across the tracks past the signal box. In no more than a dozen steps she arrives. She has arrived. See Ava arriving. Town. It's like the air is different. There are people all over the place. Hapless pedestrians, commuters racing for the city train, poor mute fools, when will they learn? She is a social animal, no longer alone. (Is that Rousseau?) She barely registers the exertion in her lungs. Or the fact that her armpits are damp. She's fit for an old bird. Puffing a bit. Thinking in short sentences. The town is waking up. The company of her peers. Or is that conspiracy? And no, not peers, if truth be hinted at, it's the company of her species, those ill-used victims, like talking with parrots, or trying to converse with ants about the meniscus of the honey jar. Even that is stretching it a bit. Only yesterday did she feel a tingly sensation of communion with one of her fellows, a shivery feeling of unity. Was it only yesterday? It could well come again. We are one, you and I. I am you; our thoughts are attuned, she had thought, only to find it was a complete misunderstanding about the ingredients of her sandwich. Not cucumber at all. God, how they laughed. She wonders if she can recapture that again, that fleeting sense of harmony. Why?

Because it felt nice. Horripilation. The melancholy of hope. Today's likely outcome. No! Banish that thought. Replace it with *munificence*. The munificence of hope.

The shops are just opening for business, stirring the night air within. Shop girls bringing out signs and billboards onto the footpath. Last-minute schoolchildren running for the bell down the hill to St Canice's. Buckets of flowers outside the florist's. Macarthur's Electricals with vacuum cleaners of all shape and size in the window ... *Clearance Sale ... Half Price ... Everything Must Go ...* All this literature! In a nearby café the chalkboard sign: *Feeling peckish? C'mon in ...* Yes, she is feeling peckish. And there is still plenty of time, a whole day in fact. Ava opens the door – she has to give it a little weight – and goes into the tea shop. The window seat is free. She takes her usual table, where she can watch everyone go about their business and, more importantly, they can watch her. What could be more harmless? A woman taking her morning *café au lait.* She can be conservative. She can play that game. She takes a seat and lays her machete in its scabbard across the table. She peruses the cardboard menu, playing the part of a woman perusing a menu. A bus pulls up outside the café and disgorges a gaggle of early-morning tourists. Don't see as many of them about these days. Must be the weather. Ava glares at them. Don't they care that it's winter and they should be somewhere warm? They're disrupting her view of the street, crowded together like ducks in a puddle.

The waitresses behind the counter whisper to each other. One of them, a girl called Marjorie, Ava rekindles the story in her mind, has just finished an assignment for uni and has been dropped off at work by her paternal parent. The assignment is about Immanuel Kant's notion of *apriori* knowledge transcending the bounds of experience, but that is really beside the point. The manager has ticked her off for being late again and Marjorie worries that she has clocked up too many negatives in her short career at the café. This is the scenario Ava has imagined for her. It may well be true. Marjorie does not dislike this job. She needs it. The shifts are flexible, which helps with her lecture timetable. The money is adequate. No, Ava edits, the money is brilliant. It's close to home. Her black skirt has not been washed and she hopes that the manager does not notice this dereliction of duty. She hasn't had time. There are floury handprints on her apron. And now the first customer of the day is this funny old woman, the same one who comes in every other morning sitting in the window seat. She hopes they can get the ingredients right today. Marjorie sighs, from exasperation as much as the impression it gives that she is working hard.

While Ava settles herself the second customer of the day comes in after her. It's a young lad; Ava's never seen him before. He's got the wispy straggle of the first attempt at a beard. What's the point of that, Ava wonders. If you can't grow a fully fledged, starling-hiding bush of a beard then why bother? Something you could lose your keys in.

'Hi, Mitch. Late again,' says Marjorie.

'Yeah, the boss'll be fuming, but I can't start the day without a coffee.'

'Big night last night?'

'Nah.'

They obviously know each other, Ava deduces. The boy, Mitch, spills coins on the counter to pay for his coffee. He's late for work. Ava can conjure a whole scenario for him too. A whole crowded universe. They lower their voices and Ava can no longer eavesdrop, as fine-tuned as she is with that activity. Writer at work. She can see Marjorie is flirting. She remembers flirting. She can also see that Mitch is completely oblivious to that behaviour. It's an entire lifetime's romance nipped in the bud. Strangled by its own umbilical cord. The young won't be rescued, she reminds herself, irrespective of the pearly words of wisdom she may or may not have to offer. The young only want to be the centre of everything. And the centre of everything is the eye of the maelstrom.

Ava takes off her pith helmet and lays it across the machete. A coil of her hair springs up. The salt shaker is fuller than the pepper cellar. She opens the sugar bowl and, taking a pinch, pops the grains on her tongue. Then she does the same with the salt. Some of the tourists outside on the street open the café door to the tune of a small bell. *Ting-a-ling-a-ling.* Ava knows she should order quickly, otherwise she'll have to wait for ages for these raggle-taggle gypsies to make up their minds as if they have all the time in the world. Mitch is already taking up enough of her oxygen. Communion with her fellows? Not yet. She raises her arm and signals to the waitresses. They are like a pair of Siamese twins tearing themselves apart with the sound of crepe paper. Marjorie wanders over. The tourists gaze up at the chalkboard menus, concentrating as if they are choosing between the doors to Heaven or Hades. It's not brain surgery, for goodness sake, it's only a sandwich.

'Morning, Ava.'

'Good morning, my lovely,' says Ava. 'Now, what will I have? Hmm.'

'Tea?' Marjorie offers helpfully. She glances back at Mitch at the counter.

'Tea. Yes! Capital idea. Tip-top. You're a mind reader.'

Ava's doing a good job of disguising her impatience.

'It's what you have every morning.'

'Is it? You saucy minx. All right, I accept your suggestion. Bring me tea.'

'And toast?'

'Yes. Toast as well. I bow to your experience.'

O bright Parnassus, Ava thinks, as Marjorie wanders off to her duties, her hair hanging down behind like a spray of autumn sunlight. How gorgeous the young look, especially from the back when they don't know you're looking. Like creatures from the thick of a coral reef. She tries to think back to the time when she had buttocks like that, but it's too long ago.

'And don't forget the jam.'

She notices Mitch take his cup of coffee and wave goodbye to Marjorie (he calls her Marj), and head towards the door.

'Bye, Mitch,' Marj carols after him. There is a whole chapter and verse of innuendo in the look that passes between the two waitresses. Ava is a bit jaded with that. She gazes out the window. The tourists have dispersed like butterflies over a field of lavender. In a hurricane – may as well add that detail, she thinks. She studies the faces in the street on the off-chance a stray publisher might be passing by. Someone she might recognise. *My goodness, is that Ava Langdon sitting there? How fortuitous. Good morning. And what's that you happen to have in your calico bag?*

No one. Just the usual familiar strangers scuttling across the creaking floors of their ever-pressing livelihoods. Bankers, firemen, secretaries. Bakers, real-estate agents, publicans. The numb mechanics of the world's turning, illusory shield held up against death. A couple of sparrows squabbling in the gutter over some nondescript crumbs, they're just as important. A paper bag blowing across the road in a puff of wind. The whole shemozzle breathing as one being, like some great, rolling seed tumbling about looking for a pot to sprout in. Life going on. And Ava observing it from the unassailable fortress of herself. How to describe that seed, those sparrows, the inner life of that fireman? Did she bring any money? Don't say she forgot to bring her wallet. No, here it is in her pocket with today's ration, a handful of coins in her pocket too. Her contribution to the national economy, the survival of the ant hill.

Where was she? The anonymous hero overseeing the trials and traumas of her people. Anonymous or eponymous? Her people, nevertheless, going about their business of being ants.

'Your tea, Ava.'

Back in the tea shop, Ava starts.

'Sorry,' says Marjorie. 'Didn't mean to startle you.'

The honeyed waitress at her elbow, eyeing the machete warily, plonking (ever so nicely) the cup and saucer down on the table. Music of the spoons. Also, a little silver teapot, plus a side plate with two slices of toast, a dab of butter, a splodge of jam.

'Toast. And jam.'

'I thought I ordered honey.'

'No, I'm sure it was jam.'

'You're doing it to me again, you naughty girl.'

'I wrote it down.'

She holds up her notepad. Exhibit A.

'That's not writing. That's just brain cells drying up.'

Ava can see the girl is perplexed, but there's no time to explain. She must cross-examine.

'Show me.'

'It's fresh,' says Marjorie, showing Ava the order. 'I just wrote down what you said.'

'And who is "Sam"?'

'Pardon?'

'Does that not say "Sam"?'

'No. Jam. That's a J.'

'Ah, there's your solution then.'

All these words – the humming of the vespiary. If there were no words to describe it, would it be worth living? Wouldn't life be rather going through the motions, like ants or wasps or moths. Do ants, for instance, feel injustice? The outrage of being swept up with the toast crumbs. Cognisance is everything, though without it, Arcadia. Sometimes Ava feels like her brain cells are dying, though not today.

'Thank you, my dear. Might I trouble you for some hot water?'

'Sure.'

Marjorie escapes. She clears another table and wipes it down. Perhaps she feels lucky to have got away so lightly this morning. Sometimes the old duck chews her ear off for half an hour, prattling on with her nonsense. She mustn't forget to bring the water.

Ava twirls the teapot three times in a clockwise direction, three times anti-clockwise, just to keep the world in balance. She pours. Dash of milk. *Dab, splodge, dash.* Stir the sugar. The first sip – *ahh* – and all is right with the universe. She inhales the aroma. O the glorious cups of tea. Panacea for every ill. Calm hiatus. All harm held in check. She can feel the harmony oozing through her brittle old veins. She tops up the silver pot with the hot water, steeping every sixpence's worth of tannin out of those tea leaves floating in the water like bloated ants. Do ants bloat? She has to say she has never seen a bloated ant. The injustice of it.

Marjorie goes about her duties, watching from behind the counter, her stockade. It's quite a performance, not least the twirling of the pot, the rituals with the toast cutting, each slice divided into quarters. An egg would have been an adventure, except Ava did not order an egg. Or did she? She chews methodically. She drains the pot. She licks the little jam dish. She catches the eye of the waitress, the tall one with the legs.

'*L'addition, s'il vous plaît,*' Ava calls, almost snapping her fingers, but thinking better of it. Poor girl, just trying to make a buck like everybody else, even if she doesn't know what a well-cooked egg is. Marjorie shrugs at the French and brings the bill. Ava spills a handful of change on the table and counts out the coins like someone trying to weigh their life in grains of rice. She still can't get used to this new money. New to her. Dollars and dimes, it's all so American. She doesn't want to be diddled and needs to be circumspect until her next royalty cheque arrives. Happy days. Then she'll splash out. Wait and see. Champagne for everyone!

Well, she can't dilly-dally here any longer. She'll outstay her welcome. Her chair scrapes backwards on the wooden floor. An ugly sound. Reminds her too harshly of the hard-edged world. She dons her accoutrements. With her helmet on she squashes the genie back in its bottle.

'*Bonne chance, petite amie,*' she calls from the door, letting it slap back as if she is leaving the tent to cross the tundra. Marjorie waves, and for a moment Ava knows exactly what she is thinking. There, that's the most interesting part of the day gone, and it's barely nine o'clock. She's wondering how the old lady occupies her time and if she has any family. If Marjorie, too, might one day end up like that. Like what? Like a dowager. Marjorie goes to collect the money, correct weight, and takes it to the till in which she knows there are no answers.

Out on the street Ava feels the chill in the air. She's been sitting still too long. Her armpits are cold. She rubs her biceps. Fortified by the tea she strolls down the big hill of Katoomba Street. The street is about five or six hundred yards long. She has forgotten how many steps it takes. Shops, many of them empty (such is the state of the economy), line both sides, and sometimes in winter snow and ice make crossing the road a precarious business. Today, however, it is not snowing, although anything could happen. No longer perambulating, she is a woman on a mission. From the corner of her eye she examines the carriage of her reflection in shop windows. In the watchmaker's display she appears floating amongst clocks and timepieces. In the newsagent's she is ethereal amongst headlines. *Nixon fallout continues … First female president for Argentina …* She moves on. Next along is the baker's window fogged with heat from the ovens, smells delectable wafting out the door. What a fine figure of a man staring back at her; that machete at his waist, now that's a machete to envy, the rakish tilt of it. How many midnight panthers has she slain with that blade? What adventures. The people in the street, can they not see the readiness for action emanating from her? Her readiness to spring to the rescue. She hears a scream, but it is only a child screaming, distraught at the discovery that it is not the centre of the universe. Nevertheless, a scream. Its mother is trying to placate it with practised lies. It might have been a street crime where, in her mind, she leaps into the fray. It is a vision ripe for swift narration. She sees the gap-toothed purse-snatcher galloping down the street, fleeing the shrieking woman in distress, hands held in horror to her cheeks. My life savings, she cries, my child's last blood transfusion. And Ava stepping into the path of the guffawing, oafish would-be-thief, machete raised, crying *Halt!* and the youthful miscreant, tripping in fright over his own feet, tumbling to a grazed, undignified surrender at her feet, her boot pressing him to the ground, the fear in his eyes, realising the terrible error of his ways, never no never again. Ava relieving him of the purse, flamingo pink, returning it to its rightful owner. *Thank you, sir, thank you. Think nothing of it, my pleasure, madam. How can I ever? Please don't bother your pretty little … My Egbert was so frightened. This little soldier here, no I don't believe it, what a delightful child …*

Swift narration and perhaps embellishment.

She stops. Is that how that scenario would go? Something is missing. Her hat? No. Her coat? Suddenly, in horror, she realises that her calico bag is gone. The bag containing the manuscript. The manuscript containing the – O holy Jesus – the kernel of her life. Her life! She spins around and scampers back towards the café. Suddenly, like a bolt of lightning, the world is focused on that single point of meaning. Out of my way, to the ants on the street. People in fact do step aside, as if she might be dangerous. How could she have walked so far without it? She flings the door open and charges inside. There are a couple of other people sitting at tables now.

'My bag!' she cries.

People look up at the panic in her voice. They stop chewing. Marjorie is wiping down Ava's table with long even swipes. Ava still thinks of it as *her* table. The tea cup and side plate and serviette have been removed. The bag is nowhere to be seen – O damned Judas – Marjorie has replaced the cutlery and in a moment every trace of Ava's presence has been erased. Is this the world in microcosm? To obliterate people as soon as they have disappeared from sight. Where is her—?

'Did you forget something, Ava?' Marjorie asks. Ava wants to slap her, the empty-headed harpy. Playing games with the kernel of her life! Marjorie points over to the till, where the other waitress, smiling, holds up Ava's bag. O, you angel. She breathes a long, bottomless sigh.

Dear God, that was close. Ava snatches the bag and holds it to her breast. How can she have been so careless?

'Thank you, oh my God, thank you.'

'No problem, Ava. I went to the door but you'd gone. We knew you'd come back for it,' says Marjorie, holding a handful of crumbs in the cup of her hand.

'You don't understand.'

'Sure. It happens all the time. Umbrellas, jackets, all the time. One woman even left her baby here.'

'Well, you can always have another baby.'

Ava checks to make sure the contents are safe. They are. Pink and perfect. What is a baby compared to this? She turns to leave, crying out once more over her shoulder:

'Thank you, thank you.'

Out on the street she exhales another sigh of relief. Be still my beating heart, I nearly lost you. She walks clutching the bag. Talk about a lesson in the fragility and transience of everything. What if someone were to snatch her bag? It's been known to happen. Someone could knock her off her feet as easy as pie. She shudders at the thought. She'll have to be more careful.

Before she knows it she's at the bottom of the hill. She's come too far. She crosses the road near the garage on the corner and starts to march back up the other side. A pigeon brushes past her face, flying under the shopfront awnings. It lands with a flutter of wings on a hanging sign which says *Boots*. Beneath it on the footpath is a montage of guano, speckled grey and white and pepper. Ava steps around it, off the kerb into the gutter where a passing car honks its horn at her, *beep beep*. Ava gives it two fingers. Footpath anarchy. She passes the Catholic primary school, St Canice's, where the voices of the ankle-biters belting out a hymn spill from the windows: *All things bright and beautiful.* It's a street in a town like any other. The bare trees shivering in the fleeting winter sun. The simple glory of it. She continues climbing the hill towards the red-bricked post office where her destiny awaits. Surely it must be open by now. In the sky there are several used cotton balls of clouds. She has to stop a couple of times on the way up, her pulse at a pace, a-gallop a-gallop, a trip-trap trip-trap, who's that passing over my bridge?

She climbs the steps and shoulders open the door. It is quiet inside the post office, like Aladdin's cave. *Sim sala bim. Open sesame.* The heavy door swings shut behind her, blocking out the noise of the traffic. There is a sudden hush.

'Don't panic. I have arrived,' she says to no one in particular. Panic is the last thing the chap behind the counter looks like doing. In particular there is only a little old lady in the queue before her. How do these little old ladies get so old? Ava wonders. One day they are twirling girls, or brides, or presidents of Argentina, then the next they are about to take their false teeth and their wisdom into the grave with them, give it all up to – what shall we call it? she ponders – the ether of forgetfulness. Am I such a twirling girl? Ava thinks. Was I ever? When she was younger she would have stopped and written that down – the ether of forgetfulness – now she's too tired, and already it's gone.

Ava is slightly put out at having to wait. Don't little old ladies realise the import of the pink and perfect wonder she has in her bag? All the old woman in front wants is a stamp. The stamp of a foreign queen, if you can stomach it.

38

She fiddles in her purse. People are blind to the splendour of radiance, and look, it's everywhere. They wouldn't have a clue if God stepped on their foot and said, 'Excuse me, I think I might be next.' Ava taps her machete in its sheath, holding her tongue. Eventually the old woman licks her stamp and moves aside. The post office man, whom she knows as Mr Dieter Meintollen on account of his name tag, and whose name she has homogenised to Mr Menthol on account of his fragrance, says:

'Next please.'

Another human transaction. This is how the cavemen advanced, she considers, beyond the need of skewers and cudgels. Dieter has a thin, red moustache like a sunburnt shoe lace. That must take some work. There is a little vein the size of a mosquito wriggler on his chin. Originally from Randwick – Ava imagines reading between the lines – he has just come from his modest little home, where he has tied his daughter to her bed until the unwed pregnancy, or other domestic catastrophe, is resolved one way or another. A scene ripe for unlikely intervention and rescue involving a ladder and her machete. She could follow him home. She could save the day. At least, that's what takes place inside Ava's helmet. Is it a vision or is it a plot? No, she has to learn to be more realistic. She could conjure a scenario where Mr Menthol lives alone and loves his garden more than the sum total of all humanity. His freesias especially.

'Good morning, good fellow,' says Ava. 'I've come to check my mail.'

The man stares at her, and eventually speaks.

'You know you can't bring that knife in here.'

'What knife?'

'That knife.' He points to her thigh.

'You'll thank me for it one day,' says Ava with confidence.

'What do you mean?'

'Who would foil the great post office heist when it happens? And it will. It's inevitable. Now, about my mail.'

'Name?' asks Mr Menthol.

'You mean you don't recognise me? Ah, I see you don't. Langdon. Ava Langdon.'

Ava shows him her profile, the yellow cravat at her throat like a bloodthirsty budgerigar. He studies her without expression.

'The same Langdon that was in here yesterday?'

'None other. Was that impertinence I detected in your voice, sir?'

'Not from me it wasn't. Would you like me to go and check.'

'Nothing would exacerbate my pleasure more.'

Surely Menthol can't be his real name. Dieter passes through the swinging door and disappears out the back. This is where Ava's imagination has to take over.

In the back room Dieter fills the kettle with water and pops it on the stove. She sees him get a cup down from the cupboard and spoon a generous amount of instant coffee into it. One sachet of sugar. He has worked out how to take advantage of being invisible. On the windowsill a clay pot with the dormant corm of a freesia in it. Presumably freesias have come to symbolise something – what exactly Ava can work out later. Nothing in the mail basket. Sacks of yesterday's letters waiting by the door for the truck. His packet of cigarettes (mentholated) waiting for him also. Only so much time can be spent out here, Ava deduces, without raising suspicion.

What on earth is he doing? She finds herself staring at the various posters and advertisements on the walls – *Passport Applications*, for instance – the smooth, burnished wood of the counter, the scales for weighing parcels. She wonders if she can lean over far enough to reach the cash drawer. Behind her a slant of sunlight creeps in through a window.

Eventually (she's feeling mean-spirited) the ginger moustache and its host Dieter return.

'Nothing today,' he says.

'No? That's a disappointment. I was expecting something from my publisher. Angus & Robertson, perhaps you've heard of them? A missive.'

'Really,' says the impudent fellow.

'Yes, really. Would you mind terribly checking under my other name? That is if you're not too predetermined.'

'Eh? I can check, I suppose. What's the name again?'

'Wilde. Oscar Wilde.'

'I beg your pardon,' says the fellow, his eyebrows raised to the heavens like a couple of leeches smelling blood in the vicinity. It is the usual reaction. People never believe her when she utters the truth, which is why she is prepared like a good girl guide. Ava takes from her bag the official deed poll certificate of name change which the department of changing names has sent her. What is that department called again? Yes, that's it, the Department of Nomenclature. She carries it for identification, not just for proof of existence. Here it is. She taps out with her finger the title for the clerk to read plain as day. *Oscar Wilde.*

Yes, he has heard correctly. He recognises all the officialdom of the certificate.

'Wilde,' he says. 'I'll go and see.'

Ava's reverie follows him through the swinging door. His cup. The kettle hasn't boiled yet. It feels like she's in two places at once.

Meanwhile Oscar folds away the certificate. It's a certified copy, one of many, signed by a Justice of the Peace, if you please. Again the posters, the dusty sunlight, the scales. Yes, the cash drawer is out of reach. She puts out a finger and presses the scale plate, watches the needle fly around several chaotic kilograms. The trespass feels delicious.

Dieter and his leeches return: 'Nope. Sorry.'

'That's a relief. Now, on another matter, I wish to procure a *sac postal.*'

'What's that?'

'An envelope. Plus postage. This is a post office. You are the postmaster. I don't mean to tell you your job.'

'What do you want to post?'

'This.'

Ava opens her bag and extracts the parcel from which she pulls the hefty manuscript in its two rubber bands. She lays it on the counter. She can feel the heat radiating off it. Four hundred pages. Four hundred and one, actually, if you count the cover letter. Single spaced. Pink as a newborn rose. Her eyes positively sparkle. What a journey they've been on together.

'That'll cost a bit.' He doesn't look surprised, as if people come in every day to post *great works*, post them by the truck-load, putting themselves at the mercy of the universe, no, the *service* of the universe.

'The cost is irrelevant.'

Mr Menthol reaches out a hand to take the bundle in his nicotine-stained fingers.

'What are you doing?' Ava squeaks, snatching it back.

'I have to weigh it.'

'Oh, yes, of course.'

She lets him take the manuscript, not taking her eyes off it, nor her casually placed hand off the machete's hilt. What if the world were to end right now? What if a meteor were to hit the post office? What loss. What a vacuum. So if she has to take his hand off at the wrist she is ready. He centres it on the scales. She is interested in how far the dancing needle goes.

'Just under two kilos.'

'Goodness.'

Think of that. She thinks of that. The clerk selects a large parcel-envelope and, after assessing the weight, hands over the appropriate bevy of multi-coloured stamps. Ava pays. The commercial pecuniary aspect of it is straightforward. It's a cost she has factored in.

'Bring it back to me when you've finished addressing it.'

'Thank you, *garçon*.'

She can smell the osmidrosis off of him like the tang of green bacon. A part of her wonders if it might be her. The smell of her organs rotting.

Ava turns away. She takes the envelope and her parcel, her latest, greatest work, to the privacy of a far counter beneath a window. There is a line of fat and skinny telephone books along the bench. Two kilos of radiance. Her kneecaps tremble with excitement. One last look to check that everything is in order.

She stares at the title page with vague anticipation. *The Saunteress.* The plain font is beguiling as to the marvels contained within. Perhaps she should take the whole bag of brilliance home and read it again? What if one of those wait-resses has got the pages out of order? At random she lifts about a kilogram of it and, turning it like a wave in the mottled sunlight from the window, reads:

… from the bright surface where the ducks raked their feathers with quiet pride. The long hose pipe of the pump sucked river water through its great peristaltic intestine and, travelling via a complicated system of pipes and conduits, fanned it out over the orchard in a dizzying mist. Half-a-dozen rainbows flirted above the tree tops, vanishing and reappearing as the sprinklers revolved. The birds, cockatoos and crows mostly, flew through the arcs of isolated rain and threaded them together in a dance beyond my understanding. It was like some glorious music box, a chandelier circling in the air. The heat of the morning was powerful and I was torn between throwing myself in the river, wantonly, clothes and all, not caring who might be watching, or a more immediate, primal urge. Hunger.

'Come on, Red,' I said, 'I'm hungry. Engels won't miss us.'

'Let me just finish this sack, Dave.'

The river could always come after, so now, while Engels was away, we wandered through the orchard towards the watermelon patch on the far side overlooking the wide Buckland valley. One of the other pickers called out from his leafy perch:

'Where are you two off to?'

'None of your ear wax,' I rejoindered. They all jealously wondered what adventures we got up to. Our elevation above the menial. Our shoulders felt free from the weight of the apple sacks, free as if our wings had been torn out by the roots and, for the moment, we enjoyed a priceless, immortal freedom. The quiet voices of the pickers drifted through the leaves. Several unused ladders stood akimbo in the grass. In the untouched trees apples hung suspended in the air like Turkish lanterns. A couple of days of hot weather would bring them on nicely, and Engels would shift us over to pick this corner of the orchard. In a number of these trees dead cockatoos hung strung up by the necks, shot by Engels as a warning to other birds to touch his apples at their peril.

The melons lay on their sides, fattened piglets asleep in the sunshine. They were warm to the touch, and echoed with a hollow, corky sound when we rapped our knuckles on them. Rat-a-tat-tat. Red chose her melon and I selected a fine specimen still attached to the ropy vine by its umbilicus of stem. A fine melon, a rambunctious melon, the sort of melon you'd give to Caesar on his birthday, royally pale underneath where it lay on the dirt, like a shark's underside. Neither of us had a knife. We broke the stems and raised our melons overhead not unlike Abraham hoisting Isaac high unto God's silver platter. But there was no God. No mighty voice to stay our hand. Only us and the golden sunshine and the river defined by a line of trees in the distance. And the sacrifice that was rightfully ours. Down we threw them and smashed the melons on the fertile earth. The melons broke into several pieces. Red and I each picked up a chunk of flesh, sun-stunned, warm as blood, and buried our faces in the sweet, juicy pulp. We drank. It was like drinking champagne sunlight, or like being kissed by the purring Queen of the bees fresh from winter sleep, the fruit so sweet and delicious. We sucked as if it was the sun's blood and we ate and when we pulled the melon husks off our faces the juice ran down our chins and throats, dripping on our manly chests. We spat the seeds at each other. God how we laughed. Red had watermelon seeds in her hair, and I suppose I did too. It was the sweetest means by which to quench a thirst I could ever have imagined. Then we went and washed our hands and faces in the river. Our clothes, we knew, would dry in next to no time. Afterwards we strolled back to the orchard to start picking again. The trees were calling us. The rumbling music of apples tumbling into bins came to us on the air, a murmured dialogue, like two lovers talking quietly at dawn. As we walked up the row we each plucked the most perfect example of appledom we could find and, after polishing them on our bibs, took a big, horsey crunch. Engels, the boss-cocky, was waiting where we had left our ladders and picking sacks, our bins half full.

'Where the heck have you two been?' he demanded.

'Not your affair, friend,' said Red, munching her apple with big beautiful tombstone teeth that filled her heart-shaped mouth.

'Those apples won't pick themselves, you know.'

'Keep your hair on,' I interjected. 'Aren't we allowed to have some lunch?'

'It's not lunch time. Lunch from twelve-thirty is.'

'Oh, give it a rest, you silly nit,' I said.

Boss-cocky Engels was an annoying fellow. About as fat as a match with an accent you couldn't quite place. He had a funny little moustache like a toothbrush which did him no favours at all and did not endear us to him. We wondered if it was a fake and whether he peeled it off at night and kept it stuffed up his nose like a mouse in its lair. I bent over to pick up my sack when all of a sudden he was on me breathing his fried breath. It must have been the last straw for him.

'Don't you talk with me like that.'

'Get your hands off me, you drongo,' I said.

'I'd go a pound or two for a round or two with you any day of the week, Dave, at the drop of a hat. You see if I wouldn't. I—'

But before he could progress further with this fine speech I clocked him one full on his proboscis and sat him down hard on his btm. He went down like a proverbial pile of bull's droppings. Blood sprayed from his nose like the Rose of Tralee, like rust-red river water fanning from the sprinklers over the orchard. I stood over him like Cassius Clay over

Sonny Liston and the force of my gaze kept him pinned to the ground. Bluebirds seemed to flit in orbit about his head. Red was grinning from ear to ear and looked more beautiful, standing there in the sunshine, than I had ever seen her. She was nineteen.

'There, Engels,' I said, 'how do you like that from a girl?'

She looks up and breathes. Her pupils bright sparks. The sprinklers and their rainbows slowly fade from their illumination swimming through the vitreous humour in her eyes. What magician has transported her here to this dusty post office in Katoomba on a winter's day? She has been elsewhere. She'd not be surprised to find an apple in her pocket. She turns another page and her attention is caught by something Dave has written:

Give me a glass of poison of the true vintage
Peppered with piss and aloe and tomato sauce,
I'll toss it down with a cyclopean grimace
And the lilies will sprout from my dainty corpse.
The pure, cool bloom of raw despair
Flies from me like an undisputed fact
And I am found. All hope is here
In the lancing of truth's blind cataract.

Fine sentiments for an apple picker, she thinks.

Ava taps it all together and slides the manuscript back into the parcel and closes it. The rubber bands, the cover letter. Everything into the large, heavy-duty envelope on which she now prints the address. (She knows it off by heart, just as she knows Douglas Stewart will instantly recognise her handwriting.) She licks and affixes the stamps, giving them a satisfying thump with her fist. The taste of the gum is not unpleasant. It is the taste of adrenaline and of possibility, which is how, in her heart of hearts, she would like to face every day. That is, bravely, proudly, resolutely. She turns and takes it back to the clerk. Dieter Dieter onion eater. There are now several people in the queue before her. Where did they come from? She is happy to wait, holding her baby, wallowing in the future. She shuffles forward. The time has come to say adieu. When her turn arrives to yield it up, the clerk seals the envelope, punches it with his date stamp. She watches him place it in a tub to await the postal truck and the practical, esoteric magic that will whisk it away and transform it into a tome. A monograph. A legacy.

'Goodbye, dear creature,' she says. And old Menthol, not sure, she thinks, if Mr (or Mrs) Wilde is addressing him, or the parcel, or the human condition in general, anticipates his coffee break with disproportionate enthusiasm.

* * *

Ava steps out the door feeling significantly lighter. Two kilos lighter. Fancy that. The weight of her wings. She smacks her hands together. Her task is done. She confronts the red post box outside, the one invented by Anthony Trollope, so that's surely a happy omen. She circles it three times in one direction, then three times in the other. The spell is cast. *Voilà!*

Now she has the whole day to get through, and yet no

responsibility. Her spirits are lofty, like flying buttresses. What else does she have to do on her list? Damn it, she has forgotten the list. Let's see if she can remember. Her novel has gone; that's the most important thing. It's now in the lap of the gods, or at least winging its way towards the lap of the gods. She sends blessings after it. She is two kilos lighter, therefore what she needs – yes – is a new ream of paper.

She executes a turn of the town looking for the newsagent, the one who specialises in her brand of paper. She finds it where she left it and the proprietor, Mr Gordon Shoebridge, has one ream of pink paper left. Lucky last. She wonders who else is buying all the pink paper. There's been a bit of a run on it, like a commodity share price. A part of her contemplates shoving the ream into her bag, or up her shirt, and making a run for it, but the last time she did that she had to languish in the police lock-up for two days until Douglas Stewart was able to get away from his desk and bail her out. She's learned her lesson. *Sorry, Your Honour, won't happen again.* Good old Doug. It might be stretching a friendship to call on him again for a similar misdemeanour so soon.

It wasn't just the paper. It was worse than that.

She remembers that day in the library marching up and down the aisles of tomes, all hardbound, mummified in plastic. Neither of her books could be found. She asked the librarian if, perchance, they had both been borrowed. The librarian had never heard of them. *The Apple Pickers* nor *The Golden Cravat.* Perhaps the latest bestseller would do to satisfy her reading needs. Ava spat – *Pah!* Wouldn't know literature if it bit them on the arse. (She was angry that day.) In the general fiction section Ava discovered a well-thumbed edition of the latest bestseller. One million copies sold! *Pah* again! She cracked the book open at the spine, knew just where the join was weakest. She laid it open like a sacrificial goat on the carpet, hidden between the shelves of books. Then she unleashed her machete, samurai-warrior style, and raising it above her head brought it down, and cleaved the book in twain, splitting it down the middle like a coconut. And that was when, seeing the scimitar rise again, the librarian screamed. A young policeman came and hauled her away. Ever since, the library has been a kind of Cuba to her, even though she told them that she knew how to repair the book. It's a dying craft and she'd have been happy to teach them. They declined.

Following this, Douglas Stewart, famous poet and editor, sacrificed a fair bit of his time and patience bailing her out. He'd had to catch the train up from Sydney when there were so many other needy poets after his attention. Meanwhile Ava languished in solitary. No one would listen to her confession, and one or two other drunken women refused to share a cell with her.

'No more, Ava,' Douglas had said once the papers were signed. 'No more.'

He left her at the station with a few dollars to tide her over.

So she will not make a nuisance, much as she reserves the right to. She will not cause a scandal. No fuss. Not for Douglas. Leave anarchy on the footpath. All she's after is some paper.

So she pays. It's in her budget. It is, God forbid, tax deductible. It makes her feel like an upstanding citizen, and there's something to be said for that feeling. A right and proper member of society. Mr Shoebridge remembers very well who she is and keeps an eagle eye on her. To him she's as bad as the shoplifting schoolboys. Ava imagines his home life, but then dismisses it as beneath her, at the present. He has a system of convex mirrors set up so he can see behind magazine racks and around corners if people are letting drop his merchandise into their cavernous pockets. Nevertheless, he is happy to take her money.

Ava resists temptation. With the new ream in her bag her weight, if not her equilibrium, is restored. Held to the chest, two kilograms over her heart, it would stop a bullet, she reckons, if someone were to take a pot-shot at her. It would probably stop a bazooka.

Next stop, the paint shop. She wanders down the hill again accompanied by her wading reflection. Again she gleans an impression from the periphery of her eye of how striking she must appear to the other folk on the street. Yet how few of them realise what a champion they have in their midst, simply strolling about, taking the air. A *flâneur*. A raconteur, a storyteller recording her time and place in history. Another part of her doesn't give a fig what people think. Although, she wonders, perhaps fame has abandoned her; her moment in the light, gone – that twinge of doubt like a cloud passing over the sun. She looks up. There is a cloud passing over the sun, but it is only a cloud, not a symbol. Not a psychic eclipse. Clouds do that all the time. Her manuscript is in the mail. Winging its way. She is free. Life is, you'd have to say, almost unbearably good.

In the art shop – *Framing, Easels, Palettes, Brushes, Maulsticks* – she buys a tube of Armanth Red and another of Dark Byzantium. Her tubes at home are getting a bit wizened, like old potatoes in the bottom of a cupboard, or the husks of dried blowflies. The artistic side of her nature is something she has tried to encourage in recent years. The art shop proprietor, Mr Guido Guilfoyle, himself a weekend portrait painter specialising in profiles, pops the paints in a paper bag. His trouble is he talks too much about technique, which annoys the bejillikers out of her. She would like to tell him about inspiration and flashes of luminous brilliance that prevent her from sleeping, but he doesn't seem interested. He thinks real art stopped at *Whistler's Mother*. Look at that nose, now there's a nose. He gives her the change and she counts it. It's been an expensive day and it's not over yet. Some days are like that. You have to grin and bear it.

She wishes there was a gun shop in Katoomba whose window she might ruminate and daydream before, in a fashion she approves of, to while away some time. Why? Because she does so love guns, they make her feel almost weak at the knees, but there is no gun shop. The grog shop will have to do. She doesn't know what time it is, exactly, only that it's about time for a snifter, a celebratory toast, a hair of the werewolf.

The sky is slowly filling with cloud, yet the light is clear, clear as chicken soup. Ava strolls, taking the air. She finds herself outside the early opener, Blackburn's Family Hotel on Bathurst Road. What led thou thus to mine door? It's like her feet have minds of their own. She debates with herself whether the front bar, with its smoky, acrid, mindless smell of men, will treat her with the regard the day deserves. Or not. She does not like it when, on occasion, they have howled her down and called her names. Bugger them. Will her accomplishment be truly comprehended? Or will they merely humour her, try to persuade her out to the snake-pit with all the other sorry wives of pisspots. But then, it's early, so she goes in. Begone all mine enemies. And they are. The front bar is empty. There's not even a barman. The dark timber of the beams and walls absorbs all light from the door so she has to let her eyes adjust. This carpet has seen its fair share of fisti-cuffs over the years. She hums a tune to herself. *Hello-o.* She looks at the photos on the wall of the victorious Katoomba cricket team from last year and the year before that. There are other photos of the racing cars carving up the peace around the swamp in Catalina Park. *The Gully,* they call it, another sacred place usurped. She coughs and jingles the coins in her pockets. *Yoo-hoo, anybody ho-ome?* No one comes. She spills her jingling coins on the counter, then sweeps them up and spills them again with the sound of Hell's doorbell.

'Ahoy,' she calls.

Eventually she attracts the attention of the barman, a hirsute lad called Jimi, who appears from somewhere bearing a pair of multi-grips. It's still maintenance hour.

'Sorry, mate. Just changing the keg. What can I get you?'

Ava turns her face to him.

'I'm sorry, ma'am, I thought you were a fellah.'

'An honest mistake,' she says. 'And perhaps one to profit by.'

'Eh? How can I help you?'

'A schooner of your finest, Jimi.'

'Really?'

'This is an 'otel, is it not? Of course really.'

'It's still pretty early. I've gotta hose out the gents.'

'Ah, the barman as moral arbiter, there's a nice little paradox. It's not early to me; I've been working the night shift. Autonomy of the will, Immanuel Kant would say, a time and a place for everything, and I say no time like the present, no place like here, so are you going to do the job for which you are handsomely remunerated or do you want me to keep chawing your ear off, as they say.'

'Manuel who? I don't know him.'

'Never mind. To revert: a schooner. Please.'

'Would that be a Resch's?'

'A Doctor Toohey's,' she corrects him.

'Sure.'

He pulls her drink. What a windbag he thinks, she thinks. Anything to shut her up. *Moi?* He takes the proffered money. Commerce reduced to its fundamental elements. Ava can see it all. Haggle, barter, beg. Didn't need all that palaver, just a little patience while Jimi worked it out. Humanity survives, as do the gastropods.

She finds a quiet spot in a shadowy corner. Actually the whole place is filled with quiet spots, it's one big quiet spot, but she likes the subterfuge of a darkened corner. The third man. A smuggler's cove. Umbratilous, there's a handy word. She sips. A sonnet comes to her, fully formed, but she has nothing to write it on. Well, she has the new ream but she cannot bring herself to break the seal. That act requires more considered ritual. Besides, she has no pen. Hopefully she'll be able to remember it.

While she is drinking, trying to memorise her opening couplet, the door opens to reveal a strange apparition. Already? So soon? At first she thinks it's an astronaut. He's wearing a silver space suit, the light from beyond shining all about him in a morning penumbra. He has a large, round, hairless, alien sort of head. The light bounces off it. Ava does not move. She's hidden in shadow. She eases the brim of her helmet down low over her eyes. The figure (which for some reason reminds her of Engels) steps into the gloom of the bar and stands there. Slowly he, for it seems to be a he, there being no breasts or Golden Fleece to speak of, rotates on the spot, not seeing her, not seeing the barman, quite the automaton, a full half-circle and leaves the way he came in. The door pulls itself shut. Ava can see the head is actually a motorcycle helmet, not an alien skull. The strangely familiar form disappears. Nevertheless it is a weird moment and she wonders how she might weave the image of it into her next narrative, the one lying dormant in the new ream of paper in her bag. She can't wait to get home and unleash it. However, that is an anticipated pleasure and she has learned how to delay gratification. She must exercise restraint, let the steam build up. All the precious moments of the day before that happens.

Jimi the barman catches her eye across the room and shrugs. He's no more in the know than she is. Strange figures every hour of the day and night in his world. Ava shrugs back. Bugger it, the sonnet has gone. Something about the shade. In a gulp she finishes her drink, wipes the froth off her lip with the back of her hand, and rises. She waves farewell to Jimi, who gives her a salute. She leaves the front bar and goes round the side of the building to the bottle shop. A little bell tinkles above her head as she enters. In a moment there is Jimi from within, now playing a different role. People are so versatile, she thinks.

'You again,' he says, unsurprised.

'Me forever and for always.'

'Look, love, I'm just trying to do my job.'

'Something for which I would offer you eternal encouragement.'

'What would you like?'

She buys two bottles of Penfolds Sweet Sherry. Nectar of the proverbials.

'Thank you,' she says.

'You're welcome,' says Jimi.

'There, see, it's easy, isn't it.'

She wanders back along the street, the railway station on her left, past the Niagara café to the corner and, hard-a-starboard, down the hill again, past the various heathen churches, the school, the PO, the banks, the garage on the corner. The second journey along the same path always seems shorter than the first. Who said that? Was it Kant or was it Noddy?

At the bottom of the hill, beyond the commercial precinct of the shopping strip she makes her way to Hinkler Park, lovely and green, with its skeletal monkey bars in the shapes of aeroplanes. Why this municipal fixation with aeroplanes? she wonders. She finds a park bench by a laurel hedge and takes the weight off her legs. It's the sort of hedge the boys have secret hidey-holes inside where they hide their cigarettes and girly magazines. The palpitations in her chest are trying to tell her something; that lost sonnet perhaps. She rolls up her trousers and looks at her legs, their scars and bumps and varicose veins. She thinks: *immortality*.

Time to twist the cap off the sherry, which makes a pretty cellophane crinkling-at-Christmas sort of noise. She raises the bottle to her lips. Lovely. The luv-erly lava boiling in her belly. She sips again and closes her eyes. The gas of satisfaction rising in her gullet. The watery sun illuminates the canals and tributaries in her eyelids thin as parchment, thin as Bible paper, lovely and pink, like maps of unknown cities. The Nile river delta perhaps, from eight thousand feet. She opens her eyes. Hinkler Park, this is where she is. It could be anywhere, she anyone, and yet it is not.

A young mother wearing a calf-length Laura Ashley dress is pushing a child on one of the swings. Presumably it's her child, although that's not guaranteed. She might be a governess. Or a kidnapper. Higher and higher, the child squeals in delight. High as an elephant's retina. Ava can see there is some sort of resemblance. The floral patterns of their clothes are not dissimilar, though that might be chance. An empty stroller stands to one side like a burnt-out tank in the desert.

Ava thinks back to her own children, long ago. Where are they now? What part of the world? She has no idea. Whom do they resemble? She has not seen the boy since he was eight years old. Would she recognise him? She remembers looking at him through a window impregnated with chicken wire.

She remembers rowing on a lake together, laughing at the ducks. It is as if her children happened in another womb, in another person. Not the shrivelled-up walnut she has in her. Like those Chinese women she has heard tell of who carry around granite foetuses inside them till they die. Children dead and ossified. Never born. A loss too great to bear. The body clinging to its grief. She has read about that. The body clinging to its grief.

She drinks. She may as well drink. See Ava drinking. She thinks, instead, about her manuscript. The glowing journey of it. Her knees start to jiggle. She cannot sit still with the anticipation. How could they not like this one? Yet, how dare they not like the others? Half in fury and half in triumph she jumps to her feet, whips out her machete and waves it in the air.

'I'll show you,' she shouts to the sky. Ava swishes her machete at the nearby laurel hedge and lops off a thin branch. Across the park the paisley woman with the child stares at her, the oscillating swing the only movement. Quickly she drags on the chain and brings the swing to an ungainly halt. The child whines at this rough treatment.

'I will not be a captive to biography,' Ava cries.

The woman hauls her child off the swing seat and marches smartly off, dragging the stroller, hauling the poor little tyke by the arm, crying now, there's injustice for you.

Ava sheathes her machete, sitting back on her bench. It's a beautiful day, even if it is starting to cloud over. Don't ruin it with imponderables, old girl. Don't get ahead of yourself. Once the mother and child have gone, Ava has the park to herself. Breathing room. She has the idea to sit on one of the swings. There's no one about; she may as well kick up her heels. It's a public park. The seat, or rather the chains at its sides, are a little tight, but she manages to squeeze into it. Made for smaller bottoms than hers. She gives herself a push backwards with her toes. Soon she has some momentum and it's like her muscles remember the routine, like riding a bicycle again after fifty years. The body remembers. She kicks her legs out and leans back on the forward swing, tucks her feet under her and tilts forward on the backswing. Back and forth like a pendulum. She goes higher and higher. Her helmet falls off and rolls on the grass. No matter. She's flying. Admittedly she's not flying very high. Even so she sees herself poised at the apex, a frozen frame from Zeno's paradox. Light flickering through the leaves. Slowing at last, every fractured moment contains the animated essence of a new person, multiple Avas, each one living a slightly different, parallel life, until at last the zoetrope approaches an impossible stillness.

And suddenly she's nauseated and seasick and has to drag her heels in the wood chips to come to a complete stop. The seasick blood rushes around in her ears. No wonder people grow out of this, she thinks, like climbing trees. Two feet planted on the ground, that's where common sense lives. Otherwise you're at the fickle whim of gravity. Ava extricates herself from the chains, gives her hips a bit of a rub. But Ava, she tells herself, wasn't it such fun. Wouldn't her sister, Red, have loved that? Leaning back, her feet touching the sky. Shouldn't all life be this state of dizzy adventure? Wonderful, fluid delirium. Isn't that what the romance of her past has taught her? She picks up her helmet and clamps it on her wind-swept hair, squashing down those contradictory thoughts, squash them down to a manageable frenzy more appropriate for a quiet suburban stroll or a picnic in the park. She strolls. See Ava strolling. Or perhaps ambling. One step at a time. There is still, at day's eventual wane, the long walk back to her hut, and the idea of that is exhausting. She has to garner her reserves. These old immortal legs don't feel quite up to it just yet.

Her hut. Home of the gods and all the wondrous figments of her past. Where her dolls line the windowsills and the cats stand guard, awaiting her return. And her books, her books. To the unknowing eye it might be construed as the yawning maw of Hell. Only she knows better. She must remember to buy more cat food. Was that on her list? Where is her list? Plenty of time for that, anyway, she thinks. As always she hopes the rats can fend for themselves in her absence. Plutus and Bacchus. So far they have lived together most harmoniously, a lesson to all, although she cannot know what they get up to while she is away. Rats, when their conversation dries up, are, naturally enough, rat-like.

Wary of the look the young mother threw her way (young mothers can be so judgemental and treacherous), Ava leaves the park and walks on. She's usually very good at walking. Picaresque, is that her style? Meandering? It's Oscar's certainly, and what she herself aspires to, but Ava is probably more agitated and driven, so the combination of the two is sometimes exhausting. She heads south down Lurline Street past the RSL club towards the escarpment. Past manicured gardens and houses the insides of which she can only imagine with a vague trepidation. What sorts of lives are being lived in there? What sorts of carpet and cutlery? It's like trying to imagine the insides of the Kremlin or the Taj Mahal. She passes a municipal council vehicle by the side of the road. A yellow backhoe and its operator are digging a hole. Or else it is a trench. What did Conrad say? *Every turn of the path has its seduction.* Now there's work to admire. They are surrounded by a makeshift fence of orange witch's hats. The backhoe man is leaning against his black-knobbed levers, looking down into the hole. Ava follows his eye. At the bottom another man is labouring away at the dirt with a spade. It's an impressive hole and Ava has nothing but pleasant envy for it, although God knows what the heck they're trying to do. Perhaps it's the sort of thing men do all the time: dig a hole, fill it in again. Entropy. That would explain the state of a lot of things.

Eventually the men realise she is watching them and a degree of self-consciousness seems to enter their work. The man in the hole stops digging. The other man on the backhoe points into the hole, but this rudimentary gesture seems to have no meaning, apart from looking authoritative. *Hole*, it declares. *Spade.* The colour of the dirt is called sinopia. She might paint this scene. *The Work of Kings.* The workmen look at her.

'Carry on, chaps,' she calls, waving regally, and, turning away, carries on herself.

She wanders, all right – saunters – down to the cliff top which constitutes, in a literal, topographical sense, the edge of town. She thinks of all the radiant ways she has described her wandering. New ones come to her. A dandy, a whirling dervish. Thoughts for later. The footpath spreads to a broader concourse like a stain across a kitchen floor. The edge of town at Echo Point is fenced in to stop people accidentally falling to their doom, or else swallow-diving off the lip of the precipice. Ava stands at the fence and swigs from her bottle. The clouds like drowned sheep in the valley. Other clouds like saintly sheep ascending to the heavens. Up there a little Cessna farts across the sky.

The view is renowned. There are a handful of tourists with their cameras at the ready, beguiled by the fleeting moment. The cold. The fact that it's a weekday. A few cars pull up and park. A buzzing motor scooter slowly circumnavigates the turning circle then buzzes away.

Along the fence another old woman leans against the wire, staring into the distance. Her hair is glaucous blue. She has a plastic rain hat on even though it is not raining. Staring, not so much into the distance, but into some purer vacancy. Ava knows that stare, where there is no horizon. Her eye sees nothing. The corneas drying in the air. It's a stare of common anguish. How would you ever know what goes on in the heart of another woman? thinks Ava. Even she who has had the writerly benefit of that conjuring is still not sure. How another person thinks? What they might see? But she can try. Is that not her charge?

Ava sidles along the fence towards the woman until they stand a yard or two apart. The clouds now like fat maggots in the valley. It's time for a demonstration of her purpose. From the woman's face, its lines and topography, Ava can see the whole unique and common story. A life in its moment. Its distinction.

In one hand Ava holds her machete aloft in praise of the spectacle that is the landscape, old Mount Solitary on the far side of the valley. In the other hand the bagged bottle of sherry.

'Salud,' she shouts at the top of her lungs.

ELEVENSES

LIMPING WITH A TERRIBLY PAINFUL perforation to the sole of her foot is how Poppy Whitaker finds herself after treading in the dark on the toy bulldozer her grandson had left on the floor. She'd yelped and even sworn under her breath – 'Sugar' – but there was no one to hear her in the middle of the night. Ava can hear it, she knows about that silence. Crying her way to the bathroom, eyes squinting in the sudden brightness, Poppy had sat on the edge of the bath no one used anymore and examined with difficulty the soft underside of her foot. When she massaged her flesh a small mole of blood appeared. The bulldozer's vertical exhaust pipe had punctured her tender fleshy arch. Why had she woken? The call of nature? No, the deafening wordlessness of nature. She splashed water on her face and examined her darkened eyes in the mirror. Exhaustion was the last thing remaining there, although she knew further sleep would be impossible. All other emotion had been drained from her. She'd had no idea how deep that pool could be, how cavernous. Beneath her weariness there was nothing but bone. The house was awfully quiet.

In the years before Theo died – Ava can imagine the pair of them – Poppy and her husband would stroll arm in arm down to the cliff tops and watch the sunsets. It was their special evening treat. In younger days they'd walk the Prince Henry walk, or the Lilianfels track, many of the others also. Poppy could say the names of most of the bird life: the Brush Bronzewing, the King Parrot, the Tawny Frogmouth, the Scarlet Robin, the Black-faced Cuckoo-shrike, the Eastern Whipbird. Ava knows nothing about birds but Poppy can tell many of them by their call. She relished the challenge of a bird call she could not identify. That would get her thumbing through her books. Theo used to tease her about it.

'Bird brain,' he'd call her.

And she'd call back, 'At least I have a brain.'

Ava wonders if there is any acrimony in the marriage, or if it floats on a more archetypal happiness.

Then he grew sick, and none of the new-fangled hospital technology with tubes going into and out of him, none of the drugs under the sun could keep him alive. The diagnosis and the prognosis, and the other terms that did not summarise who Theo was at all, they had the effect of reducing him to a 'case'. There was probably a file with a chart in it some-where. Finally, after the prolonged diminishing, the hospital told her to take him home and keep him comfortable. So they did. He was zonked out of his mind much of the time, but a part of him at least, Poppy was sure, knew where he was. Knew he was in his own bed in his own home, with his glasses within reach on his bedside table. He seemed to recognise the painting of the men pushing the funny little fishing boat out to sea that hung on the wall by the window. Paul Henry it was, the Irish painter. Theo loved that painting even though he'd never been fishing in his life. Why would a man who had never fished like fishing? Ava wonders.

One morning he told Poppy his waking dream.

'I dreamed there was a brick sitting on a wall.'

What on earth could that mean? Ava asks herself; a brick on a wall, that's not very adventurous, perhaps he made that up.

Theo recognised Denise, their daughter, when she arrived from interstate with her husband, Athol, and the kids. During one lucid period Theo made an attempt to remember their names.

Seeing him so flat and shrunken, the skin stretched over his skull, frightened the children a little, his breath often barely enough to fill his mouth. Denise encouraged them to enter the room, to ignore the smells and stuffiness and play quietly in the corner. They did for a while, then they left and could be heard running around outside, which was its own tonic. He took a sip from his mug.

'If there's one thing I've learned to enjoy in this life,' Theo said once, 'it's lemonade.'

In the early hours, it must have been Saturday morning, a Brown Thornbill was singing its first sweet notes, Theo took a deep breath, deeper than he had in weeks, and said: 'That's mine.'

Then his eyes closed and he died.

Poppy almost asked him what he meant, but she didn't.

She held his hand and sat there till morning, until Denise came in her dressing gown and, taking in the scene which required nothing of her, felt her father's cold cheek.

Ava places her hand on her own cheek, which is quite warm.

Later Denise rang the hospital. A request for the death certificate was registered. They said, with great tact and understanding, that she had best deal directly with the funeral parlour. Poppy hated that word – parlour. It made it sound like they were going to host a soirée. In turn the funeral people said they could not come until business reopened and therefore the best thing (but who knew what was the best thing?) would be to leave him laid out where he was until the hearse arrived early Monday morning. Afterwards Poppy felt hugely relieved, and grateful, that they had taken the decision (which turned out to be absolutely the best thing) out of her hands.

All weekend people came to call. Their neighbours, Theo's friends, old work colleagues from long ago, family. Poppy imagined that Denise or Athol had made a few quiet phone calls and asked people to pass the news along, like Chinese whispers, so that when they came full circle they might somehow find that the rumour was untrue and Theo had not died at all. However, the message did not change. The visitors went into the bedroom, some loitering in the doorway, and there he was, not quite sitting up, surrounded by pillows, his cheekbones prominent, but looking calm and peaceful. His mouth hung open. Denise and Poppy had changed the linen and tidied the room a bit, closing the cupboard doors, dusting the fishermen and their boat. Some of his friends spoke to him. It did not take long for the room to fill with flowers – it became quite cloying – so they had to place them elsewhere throughout the house. The few slow flies that had not succumbed to winter buzzed softly.

Another strange thing was that, once he had gone, the room seemed strangely full of subdued life, as if a wonderful meal had just been finished. The grandchildren, Rick and Sonia, took their toys in there and were happy to play on the carpet at the foot of the bed while people sat in chairs around them. For them it seemed no different a thing than if their grandpa was dozing, but usually when he dozed he had a little whistling sound caught in his nose. No one told them to pipe down. All weekend visitors came and went. They entertained in there and the atmosphere was almost quietly festive. So many cups of tea. People left curries and casseroles. When it became too much Poppy went and lay down in the study, where the couch unfolded into a spare bed.

One by one the visitors left until just the family remained to deal with the shrinking pool of things to be said. Monday morning arrived and the funeral director came with his wife. They made quite a team. They moved their gurney between the children playing on the floor, over their toys, stepping carefully so as not to break anything. Poppy left the room while they lifted Theo off the bed and placed him on the trolley. They covered him with their own special sheet and strapped him down as if he was going on a whirlwind ride at the circus. Denise saw the husband-and-wife team glance at each other and at the children.

'Excuse us now, kids.'

The children moved aside. Rick grabbed a racing car off the floor.

'Say goodbye, Rick and Sonia,' said Denise.

'Bye-bye, Grandpa,' they called.

The funeral people wheeled the trolley out of the house. Denise followed while Poppy watched from the front door. As they were sliding the gurney into the back of the unadorned hearse the undertaker turned to Denise.

'I've never seen that before. Having the children there like that. Those kids are going to have the healthiest attitude to death when they grow up.'

'Thanks,' said Denise. 'It wasn't scary. So they didn't need to be scared.'

The husband-and-wife team shook her hand.

'A good death,' said the man.

The back door clicked softly shut. The hearse drove away.

A good death.

A few days after the funeral, the house empty at last, Poppy trod on the toy bulldozer in the darkness. She picked it up and put it on the sideboard with the slowly wilting flowers, tears of a different source prickling in her eyes. The weight of Theo's head was still impressed on his pillow. The next day she decided to leave the house; that is, to get out into the open air. Alone. It had been so long. She could not stand it anymore. It was a grey, dazed morning. She did not know where she was going until she found herself at the fence at the edge of the cliff.

* * *

'Salud!' Ava shouts, and coughs solidly.

The echo returns to her. On the other side of the fence, clinging to a devil-bush, is a lace handkerchief. Right there at the slippery edge of the cliff. Surely a little girl's handkerchief. Who is there to retrieve it? Why, no one but Ava, who in her mind leaps the fence and snatches it up in her teeth, returned with a bow.

Satisfied with her echo Ava turns again to the woman beside her. She gazes for a while at the side of her face, then says at last:

'Buck up, old girl.'

The woman does not react. She has barely reacted to the echoing shout. Ava proffers the bottle in its brown shroud. Still the woman does not notice. Ava taps her on the elbow with it. Poppy starts.

'Feel like a snifter, old girl?' asks Ava.

The old woman snaps out of it. The pain in her foot twinges again.

'Oh no. Thank you. No. I.' She stops. She can't go on. Her whole life there in her face. 'It's just.'

'Yes. I'm all ears,' says Ava, all ears.

'I don't want to bother you.'

'No bother to me,' says Ava. 'Tell me all about it. Yell your lungs out. I'll let you know if you're boring me.'

Poppy takes a step away, as if to leave, but Ava follows her. 'Don't go.'

There seems to be nothing for it but to have a conversation. 'It's just,' says Poppy. 'My husband. He passed away.'

'Recently?'

'Er, yes, recently.'

'The husbands. They do that. One minute they're there and everything's smooth sailing. The next they've vanished into thin air and your happy little dinghy has capsized. Well, chin up, sister. Plenty more fish in the quagmire.'

Ava drinks. The bubbles in her throat.

'You're sure you won't – partake?'

'No. Er, no thank you. I really must—'

'Tell me, have you been blessed, and I use the term advisedly, with progeny?'

'Children?'

'Yes.'

'I have—'

'Don't. At our age they're not worth it.'

'I—'

'I'm talking from experience.'

'I don't doubt it,' says Poppy.

'Stone foetuses, all of them.'

And Poppy, astonished, seems to know what this strange woman is talking about. It's what she has too. A fossil of grief that will never go away.

Yes, thinks Ava in return, she knows what I'm on about. We can read each other's mind.

Ava would like to know her name, but cannot bring herself to ask. Instead she broaches a delicate subject the only way she knows how.

'Are you about to dive off over the fence into the eternal everlasting?'

'What? I. No. No.'

'You look as though you are.'

'I'm. No. He's only just … Recently. The funeral was last week. I'm very … We used to come here … for the view.'

'Sauntering.'

'Well, yes. I suppose. We used to like the birds.'

'How romantic,' says Ava. 'I comprehend. Tempting as that little handkerchief resting there may be, diving off the edge is no way for a woman to do it.'

'I beg your pardon,' says Poppy.

Stone foetuses are all very interesting, but this is getting a bit close to the unspoken bone of it.

'No. A woman uses her cunning wiles. Pills. Medicinals. Wisdom of the herbivores. However, if it were me I'd take a shotgun and curl my thorny old toe around the trigger and blow my lid off. Sky high! Ha! That'd show 'em. But it's never come to that.'

There is a fervid quality in Ava's voice that brings the grieving woman back to her senses. Poppy stares at her. Here she is. A woman at the fence. On the brink. Nothing but the future.

'You're sure you won't have a snifter? Call it elevenses. It'll put everything in perspective.'

The woman snorts. It is a snort halfway between a stifled laugh and a sob.

'All right then.'

She receives the bottle from Ava's outstretched hand, tips it back and takes a tentative sip. Splutters softly.

'Oh my.'

'Bracing?' says Ava. 'Against the onslaught. Not so?'

'Yes. So. Thank you, but I won't have any more. In fact, I should probably be going home.'

'Don't rush off on my account, old girl. We've only just begun to talk. And where else have you got to go?'

'Home.'

'Why?'

'I – I don't know.'

'There are no rules anymore,' says Ava.

'I suppose you're right.'

They study the sky again, each from their different point of view.

'It looks like it wants to rain,' says Poppy at last. 'I really must go.'

'Me too, old girl. Home. Last place I want to be, but that's where I'm going.'

Ava turns and dawdles along the fence line, strumming her finger along the wire.

'Excuse me,' calls the woman. Ava stops. 'Your bottle.'

'Ah, of course.'

Ava returns and takes the sherry in hand. *Salud*.

A Crescent Honeyeater calls out *e-gypt e-gypt*, from the bushes.

'Thank you,' says the woman, watching Ava's departure. 'I think.'

'My pleasure,' calls Ava over her shoulder, wandering away. Then calls:

'Clouds like maggots. Ha! Look at them. Clouds like maggots.'

Ava turns and looks back. She sees the woman, Poppy,

grief's spell interrupted for the moment, who turns towards her own home and begins, Ava can just imagine it, that new journey.

Oh, Theo.

* * *

The hole in the side of the road is still there but the workmen have gone. What a life. Don't slip in, Ava, she tells herself, you'll never clamber out again. It'll rain and fill up with tears and you'll drown dead drownded. She glances around and, feeling herself unobserved, kicks a little dirt into it. But if someone was observing, who might that person be? What entity?

By the time Ava gets back to town she is fairly bursting to go to the pissoir. She could have gone in the bushes of Lilianfels, the salubrious guesthouse, or up any of half-a-dozen discreet side streets and alleyways, all leading nowhere. She goes into the first hotel she comes across, the Clarendon. No one about. Still too early. There are pictures of hairy musicians pasted to the noticeboard, coming soon to entertain *you*. She follows her nose and stands once more before the doors of a quintessential dilemma. Male or Female. Here is her paradox. A staccato voice seems to challenge her, berate her. Hombre or Mujer. Mann or Frau. Homme or Femme. Gentleman or Lady. Come on, decide. She knows them all. She is them all. Not fluid or all-encompassing, gathering the harvest of the reaping fields, but fractured and split and bleeding. Her inner core weeping out of itself. There is nothing for hermaphrodites. It's too confusing. The words rattle around in her earbones, androgynous and humming. How can she choose?

She cannot choose. To choose is to sunder. It's like the darkness beyond the edge of the cliff. Perhaps she'll puff up with piss and pop? It's too much to ask. She decides to abandon the choice and escapes outside to the open air again. No one sees her leave. It's a private contradiction, the dark and the light, but which is which? She continues walking up the hill, the need more pressing now, *pissupprest*, it's all she can do to hold herself together, until she finds the next standard office bearer of sanctuary – a church. They're never hard to find. Here's one. Which denomination she's not quite sure, but they're bound to have a dunny! And should she split and become atoms, dispersed entirely, then God is at hand. Even priests have to piss sometime, don't they? Or is mercy a cliché?

As with the pub it takes a moment for her eyes to adjust to the darkness. It's a Catholic church. She can tell because the red light is shining outside the confessional cupboard. She wonders if that's where they keep the mops and buckets after business hours, having swept up all those spilled sins and futile salutations. She should go in, one of these days. Relieve herself – no – unburden herself. Forgive me, old sport, but I spent seven years in an asylum cursing the deities that employ you. It wasn't my fault. My husband could neither control nor contain me. I stole. I drank. I fornicated. With whom I can't remember. They said I abandoned my children. Whether I did or whether I didn't, I lived only for myself. Neither man nor woman, I'm proud of everything. I know you want more detail but that's all I'm prepared to offer up, at the moment. What peace of mind can you give me in return? Nothing; I thought so.

But she won't go in. She'll save that pleasure for a rainy day. Time is short. Time is pressing on her bladder, like a pupa stuffed in there, rank and oily, a mind of its own. She decides the red light is a sign of opportunity. God is looking elsewhere. Great big vicarious ears open to the despicable peccadilloes in the hearts of old ladies, the murderous intent as noxious as the deed. There are a few other old ducks sitting in the pews, finger-knitting their rosaries, waiting their turn to spill the beans. God be praised, she thinks, grab it while you can. Disillusionment is only just around the corner. She shuffles obsequiously – see Ava shuffling – there's the human disguise – in a simulacrum of piety up the aisle past the gory portraits of the Stations of the Cross to the door at the rear of the church; a big wooden one, leading to the priest's private *chambre d'horreurs*. Bound to have a thunderbox out here.

The door creaks open. You can almost hear the oak. Soon she finds it. WC. Anonymous. Tucked away. Gender non-descript. Any wood will do to make a signpost, as her friends the Greeks say. Hermaphrodites welcome. Ah, here are the mops and buckets. She removes her coat and unbuckles. She sits and relieves herself on the priest's throne. Unburdens. Whew. The world does not end. She is still whole. Look, a little religious homily pinned to the back of the door. One of those calendars where you get a snippet of holy wisdom for every day of the year. Today's pithy aphorism reads:

When he had thus spoken, he spat on the ground and made clay of the spittle, and he anointed the eyes of the blind man with the clay, and said unto him, Go, wash in the pool of Siloam. He went his way, and washed, and came back seeing … (John 9:6–7)

Well, there's something to think about: came back seeing. Here on the back of the toilet door. What about the deaf man? she wonders. Or the mute? Or the ignorant man? She lifts a page and reads tomorrow's maxim: *How can a man that is a sinner do such miracles?* Quite so. Or, indeed, a woman – there's the rub. There is a mauve-uddered cloud floating across a glorious sunrise. There are several boxes, square ones, of toilet paper piled up on the cistern. She pops a few into her calico bag, and a few more into the pockets of her big hairy overcoat. They'll come in handy, and God can afford them.

She pulls up her duds, arranges the braces, and puts on the coat again. It's quite a process. When she emerges the priest is standing there glaring at her, his eyebrows arched like circus tents. She starts.

She says: 'I'm sorry, Father, but confession is over for the day.'

He says: 'I think you'd best be on your way.'

'Exactly what I was thinking myself.'

'This is not a public facility, Miss Langdon.'

'You know me?' Ava asks, genuinely astonished.

'I do.'

'Well, I'm very glad to make your acquaintance. The ear of God himself. Ava Langdon.'

'Yes, yes.'

She thrusts out her hand and takes the priest's cold, reluctant one.

'Father …?'

He does not reveal his *nom de plume*. Could they be his initials on the door? Father William Congreave? No matter. Just Father, then. Even a dog may look at a bishop. Which Greek was that again? Two can play at the pithy-aphorism game.

'You know there are public conveniences in the library.'

'Don't tell me about the damned library.'

She clamps her jaw shut. She does not want to let him reduce her to anger.

'This is a private lavatory.'

'That insight,' she continues, 'somehow escaped me in my moment of desperation. I was busting, you see, Father. My bladder, you understand. I have a scybalum. A voice compelled me. Could that have been God's voice? Perhaps I should follow you into your holy cupboard over there and tell you all about my venials, my sins of omission in particular. We can haggle over a suitable penance. Would that suit Your Holiness?'

'That won't be necessary,' he says, fingering the neck of his dog collar.

'Do you know I once pulled the hair of a boy until his scalp bled?'

'This is not the time or place—'

'I'm quite prepared to recant,' she continues. 'Repent, even, and consider the possibility of joining the club, if the terms and conditions are not too onerous.'

'Please … It doesn't do to interrupt the congregants when they're trying to pray.'

'Pray schmay. That bunch of old biddies waiting to have

their wrists slapped and their bottoms tickled. Don't make me laugh, Father. I'm like to chunder all across your cassock.'

At this point the priest (whose name is surely Father William Cataract – Congreave, what was she thinking?) backs away. He can smell the sherry. Ava can read the curriculum vitae in his eyes. He never wanted to come to Katoomba in the first place. He was more than happy in Rose Bay, but the higher orders ordained and obeisance is holy, or so they tell him. Holy holy holy. By Heaven, he's annoyed at them though.

'Please, madam. Just leave.'

'Gladly, old sport.' Ava adjusts her trousers, the machete. 'I wouldn't be seen dead in a rat hole like this. Let the church stand in the churchyard, as Aristotle used to say.'

'Madam, I must insist. Your voice—'

'Fine. Fine.' Ava throws up her hands in mock surrender. 'I know when I'm not welcome. Your loss, not mine.'

She brushes past Father Cataract, who is reluctant to touch her. She throws open the sacristy door, is that what it's called? – a door at any rate – and stomps her way up the echoing chamber of the nave – listen to those floorboards – past the old biddies waiting in the gloom. Statues of Jesus in nappies, staring up the nostrils of his holy Mam. The stained glass in the high windows faded and dull, wire cages on the outside to stop people throwing rocks through them.

She calls to no one in particular: 'It's all a lie. *Spat on the ground and made clay of the spittle.*'

Ava spits on the floor of the aisle.

'There! See!'

Father Cataract trails after her looking all serene and forgiving, rolling his eyes to the women in the pews. The trials and tribulations. Don't roll your eyes at me, sport, thinks Ava.

'Goodbye,' says Father Cataract coldly from the steps.

Outside the sun is still traversing the sky like the second hand of a clock. Old Ra. Parnassus. Golden glory. The wallpaper of Heaven. That's what she's expecting. Hang on, she notes, that dew on her cheeks, it's raining. Ava holds up her face to be kissed. A sunshower. Fickle as a change of heart, butterflies touched by the fist of God. How can a sinner do such miracles? Despair and ecstasy, they're two sides of the same drachma. Anguish can strike at any time. Not too late to dash back down to Echo Point and throw herself off. There's always that option. Geronimo into the abyss. But no, get a grip, old girl, she tells herself. Calm down. That's the sort of thinking that gets you locked up behind the unbreakable glass.

She remembers when they came for her in New Zealand and interred her with sedatives and forced enemas; they tried to distinguish her thoughts from each other. Distinguish or extinguish? She can feel that sun again glowing in her mind. All is silent up in the belfry, apart from the squabbling of the pigeons, her mind leaping from conclusion to phosphorous conclusion. Calm. Breathe. Empty. So many secrets she has to keep in order to remain afloat. She can't reveal them. They're hers. There's only a hair's breadth between the fabulous and the forlorn, thin as a camel hair. While her dreams are magnificent they're a double-edged razor. If anyone were to guess, if anyone were to get too close, she'd burst into flame. Shh …

She takes a step onto the footpath. All these people on the street, are they here every day? They must be, for she recognises some of them. Yet do they recognise her? The priest did. That is the conundrum. Strangers, for all their familiarity, in this small world where everyone is isolated, held apart by the electromagnetic force of human apathy. What a phrase! Would one of them call on her, listen to her troubles, make clay from their spit and rub it in her eyes? It's not likely. They didn't come when she was locked up and needed help. They showed her her son through the reinforced glass, then led him away. The exile of the crowd. Her brain buzzes like a wasp in a bowler hat. She takes another step. Is every empty moment always this busy?

Ava looks at the traffic rumbling slowly up and down the street. It's her street, her turf. Every scrap of rubbish has a story for her: the dry patch by the side of the road, about the size of a blanket, where a car has moved off into the drizzle. When did it start raining? she wonders. The world in all its duplicity. All these things her senses have overlooked, she whose senses are normally so attuned to the machinations of the universe. A dog tied to a street sign speaks volumes to her. What might it say if only it had the powers of speech? Speak, dog. Has Immanuel Kant passed by today? Howl, mongrel, excoriate your maker. She gives the dog a perfunctory pat to which it does not respond. It's wet and miserable. Looks at her with dolorous eyes. Its owner will come back soon and then what? She smells her hand. She hadn't counted on rain, though it's light enough. She'll have to find some plastic to protect the rose ream in her bag. The rose ream.

The rose ream drags her back out of her fever of distraction that damned priest has put her to. She breathes. Back to her body and the here and now. Don't lose the purpose of the now, old girl.

Agitation subsiding she steps out and crosses the road, halting the traffic with upraised palms.

'Part, seas,' she cries.

A car slides to a halt.

'Get off the road,' grumbles a motorist out his side window. 'Do you want to get killed?'

She knows it's not worth the dignity to argue the toss with a piece of work like him. Pack away mercy for the minute; vengeance is God's. By the time she gets to the other side, not far from the Paragon café with its sprung dance floor, she is well aware, via the intermediary of the hole in her boot, just how wet the road is.

Why can't she just think *the road is wet*? Why is her brain always so fused with possibility?

The red bricks of the post office are darkening now where a downpipe has leaked over the façade. May as well go in, she thinks, and mounts the steps. The door. The dimness. All that detail.

'Never fear, I have arrived.'

The door swings shut behind her, light, dark, light, dark. Several people at the counter turn to stare, she who is dressed so extraordinarily, the cravat like a golden goitre spilling down her shirt front, the pinstripes, the braces.

'What do you want?' asks Mr Menthol, less happily this time. He looks as though he's had a busy morning.

'To enquire about the mail that no doubt awaits my perusal, gasping for air, in your … receptacle out the back.'

'Wait your turn,' says a man in the queue, a bald man with a little goatee beard as well as blond eyebrows, who doesn't bear describing.

Ava thinks she might recognise him. Then again, she might not. If this was fiction all these people would mean something, but what? It would be her job to find the meaning, to imbue life with it.

'Today's mail hasn't arrived yet,' says the clerk. Ava can see his little moustache has thickened up a bit since yesterday. Was it yesterday?

'Oh dear. I thought perchance an express delivery.'

'Nope.'

'A telegram.'

'Sorry.'

'Well, I shall have to return when they have deigned to reply.'

'You do that,' says Mr Menthol, stamping someone's letter with authority, but it's a pyrrhic victory. No one cares about his petty authoritarianism. He may as well be chained to the wall of Plato's cave.

'I shall.'

Ava turns on her heel. People are so grumpy today. She can sense the animosity towards her, the way a cat can sense electricity in the air – or is it ultraviolet light? – but to her it's like water off a mallard's posterior. Bugger them. The predator targets she who is hesitant, she thinks, therefore she will not hesitate. Mr Menthol watches her go. He still hasn't had his coffee break. The queue is endless, like the queue at St Peter's lectern. She wonders if she shouldn't dodge around the back and check for herself that the mail has not arrived. Just like a bureaucrat to tell you a lie.

Ava lets the door swing behind her, a cowpoke leaving the Lone Star saloon. She hoicks on the steps.

Outside again (all this entering and exiting, doors swinging open, light, dark, light, dark), a police car is waiting at the kerb. She recognises it from all the lights and garish colours. When she emerges, face upturned to the grey sky, one of the policemen opens his door and steps from the car, decorating his head with a smart hat. Ava loves a man in uniform and so waits to see what he has to say for himself, for he's heading straight over and it's obviously her he wants to talk to.

'Good morning, madam.'

Well, there's a fine beginning. She may as well deduce from that that it's still morning. The badge on his lapel says *Officer Fowler*. He's young enough to be her grandson. Does she have a grandson? That's another thing she doesn't know.

'Officer, what a pleasure, what an absolute delight. How can I be of assistance?'

A part of her seems to remember him from somewhere. She holds out her hand and the policeman shakes it. Ava's handshake is of the manly variety, solid and muscular, as if she's pumping a cow's teat. Bone crunching, if only she could crunch bones. What a skill that would be.

'There's been a complaint,' says the policeman. Where has she seen him before?

'I should hope so. The service in this establishment' – jerking her thumb over her shoulder – 'is certainly lacking in enthusiasm.'

'I mean a complaint about you.'

'Pray, do tell.'

'A lady in Hinkler Park has said you were waving a knife around.'

'A lady?'

'You frightened her child.'

'What child?'

'The one with her, in Hinkler Park.'

'First a lady, now a child. How the world doth multiply. What knife?'

'You have a knife at your side. What's that for?'

'You mean this?'

'Yes.'

'Well-I-never. That's for self-defence.'

'From who?'

'From dogs and other beasts of the field.'

'That's why we have a dog catcher.'

'Where?'

'I don't know at the moment.'

'That's another thing I'd like to complain about. Write that down. He's never available in my area of the municipality. I have to take council orders into my own hands.'

'Have you been drinking?'

'Only holy-communion wine,' says Ava. 'Against which there is no law, so far as I understand. I've just come from confession.'

The policeman seems to consider the likelihood of this. He doesn't want to become exasperated, but it's proved inevitable in the past when dealing with some members of the public, some members of the public who are, no doubt, well known down at the station. Ava can see his dilemma, but doesn't necessarily wish to make his burden any lighter. He knows very well where he's seen her before. They've had previous dealings. In particular, the time he was summoned to the library when she had taken this very knife and chopped a book in half for some suspicious reason. The librarian was quite upset, and young Officer Fowler had had to arrest the old lady in order to keep the peace and mollify everyone.

Despite this, he's a nice-looking boy who probably loves his work and he's not going to let her get to him.

'Miss Langdon—'

'Yes?'

'That is your name, isn't it?'

'It depends.'

'On what?'

'On the nature of your correspondence. On the alignment of the stars.'

'Listen. You can't go around town, into shops and the like, waving a knife about.'

'A machete.'

'Whatever you call it. Show me.'

'I beg your pardon.'

'Show me the knife.'

'I'm sorry, I can't do that.'

'Show me the bloody thing or I'll arrest you again.'

So much for resolve. He's sick of humouring her. She can see that now. Why does she seem to have this effect on people? Perhaps he burned his toast this morning. Started off on the wrong foot. That could explain everything. Doesn't she realise how annoying she can be? That's a very good question. Perhaps she should show him her deed poll certificate. Ava slides the machete from its sheath and hands it to him hilt first, quite the cowgirl.

'This is a dangerous weapon.'

Officer Fowler takes it and casts a pretentious eye over the edge. It's not an axeman's eye. His fingernail scratches at a scab of rust.

'Isn't she a beauty,' says Ava, eyes agleam.

'It's pretty blunt, but nevertheless,' he says, 'I've a good mind to confiscate this.'

Immediately Ava bursts into wailing imprecations. She tries to snatch it back.

'No no no no no—'

'You can claim it back at the station.'

'No. Please no. I need it. For my – I require it. Please, you can't. It's for dogs. It's my most precious – I must – I need – Please. It's – it's an antique. You don't understand.'

She wipes a tear from her eye. It's a genuine tear. Officer Fowler hesitates, holding her at bay.

'It's not for chopping any more books in half?'

'No no no no no …'

He weighs up the scene he feels she is about to cause, and the paperwork that would ensue, and the loss of an otherwise easy morning. Her face is creased with despair. It's almost comical.

'All right, all right. Put a sock in it. What's that in your pocket?' he asks.

'Where?'

'There.'

'That's toilet paper.'

She sniffs and runs the length of a finger under one moist nostril.

'What for?'

'In case I'm caught short, officer. Do you really need to ask? I have an old woman's nephritic complaint, not to mention a fistula the size of—'

'I don't want to hear about it!' Officer Fowler raises his voice along with his palm.

Ava takes a few sheets of toilet paper from one of the boxes and blows her nose into them as if she is playing the reveille. Her cheeks go red. It's a discomfiting sight and the policeman looks away. Ava expects he's wondering why all the shitty little jobs come to him. Surely he'd be happier behind a desk? It was going to be a quiet day.

She sees him glance at his partner still sitting in the car, grinning. A couple of pedestrians have paused to watch the exchange. And is that the priest, Father So-and-so, loitering on the other side of the road, under an awning? Off in search of his holy lunch. Ava spits again on the footpath – make clay of that!

'Please don't spit on the footpath,' says Officer Fowler.

'Why not?'

'Because I say so.'

'Not even if I have a fly in my mouth?'

'What sort of a fly?'

'A tsetse fly.'

A moment's thought: 'No.'

'Why not?'

'Because I say so.'

'I'm talking hypothetically here,' says Ava.

'Then hypothetically no.'

She's talking in circles. She's talking him in circles. Soon he's going to have to count to ten.

Ava doesn't know what to do with the damp toilet paper and so puts it back in her pocket. She knows they're both wondering – am I – is she – worth the hassle? We are symbiotic, thinks Ava, this young man and I: without one, the social contract collapses, the collective flies apart and all is lost. We are no more than vapour.

She takes a deep breath, preparing to explain all this to Officer Fowler.

'All right,' he cuts her off. 'This is taking far too much of my time. Listen, if I give it back will you promise not to go waving it around in public?'

Ava considers this.

'This is non-negotiable,' the young man continues. 'You frightened the little kiddie and her mother. I could have you arrested for creating a disturbance.'

'Well,' concedes Ava, 'I didn't mean to frighten anyone. I only meant to inspire.'

She scratches her chin. She notices the gun in the holster at the policeman's bony hip. So shiny and black. A part of her wonders how feasible it would be for her to pluck it out and have a look – however, there's that little press-stud she'd have to release first – and the other part of her errs on the side of caution. Though how dearly she would like to feel his bony hips.

'Miss Langdon?'

'How do you know my name?'

'Hard not to, around here.'

Ava calms down. Appeased. Flattered.

'You've read one of my books.'

'No.'

'Where then?'

'We've met before.'

'My reputation precedes me. Very well, officer. For you, I promise.'

'And when you get home take it off and leave it there. Dogs or no dogs.'

'Or else what?'

'Or else I'll come down on you like a ton of bricks.'

'Please,' says Ava, 'you can do better than that. I thought you were going to suggest you might come round to my house and tickle my toes.'

The policeman takes his own deep breath. Ava wonders, why not flirt? He's only a man after all, a simple enough creature.

'Are you propositioning me?'

'I wouldn't know.'

She gives a coquettish little turn. He quickly hands back the machete and turns to the police car where his companion has continued watching the whole charade with an amused expression. Ava sheathes the machete and wraps the wing of her coat over it like Wyatt Earp.

'Goodbye, Officer Fowler.'

Officer Fowler doesn't reply, merely slams the car door. Ava takes a step forward and fancies she can read their lips, catch their voices through the windshield.

'How's your girlfriend?' asks the driver, and Officer Fowler seems to say:

'I think she was trying to crack on to me.'

'I'm sure glad she's not my mum,' says the first.

'Yeah.'

This is what they leave her with: *I'm glad she's not my mum.* She stumbles back to the footpath, feeling desolate. Her life's zoetrope flickering from moment to moment. The heart at the periphery, there's a nice little paradox to be going on with. She spits again because she can, and the spit flies forever and is still flying.

The police car pulls out and slowly drives up the hill.

Ava looks up at the sky. Drizzle. She looks around at the street. Desolate. I am the mother of no one, and maybe that's a good thing. She looks down at the ground. *Click click click* goes Zeno's arrow across the firmament. On the footpath she spies a lost twenty-cent piece. She bends and picks it up. Beneath it a little dry patch of cement, the ghost of a coin. This is an omen, she thinks, her lucky day, and in a moment her mood is lifted. But is it the same day? Is it not another day merely repeated? Has she not already found this coin? How would you solve such a riddle? Standing there like a stunned mullet she seems, for the moment, to have exhausted her infinite options. Her choices are, in fact, profoundly limited. She could go and spend some quality time in the library, surrounded by other people's books – yes, that's where she's seen the young officer before; it all comes back to her. She knows they don't like her in there. In fact she's banned. *Persona non grata.* That's what he was referring to. Ever since she took her machete to an infuriating bestseller, right there in the general fiction section. There is nothing by Langdon, A. Nothing by Kant, I. Just all these bestsellers. She knows there is nothing like a library to puncture the bubble of a writer's sense of self-worth.

What now?

She could find another park and finish off the sherry, but then the whole repetitious palaver of her urination. These crippling rituals of the body, will they never leave her in peace? Would she just swallow sand and be done with it. In any event she will need the sherry later to keep the night at bay. For the moment she has to get out of the weather.

She hears voices, though in what language she can't be sure. At first she thinks it could be bluebirds; then it could be devils. From the primary school halfway down the hill she sees a horde of children being marshalled by a teacher up the street towards her and the railway station beyond. A horde? A throng. A lynching party. Although well ordered in two lines, all chattering at once. In English, it would appear. English gibberish. Logorrhoea. Off on an excursion. They're marching on her. Too late to scamper back into the post office. Where are the police when you need them? She cannot hide anywhere. Her heart rate is speeding up. In a moment they are all about her, like starlings, pecking at her. Or hyenas. A column either side. High-pitched chittering. She is drowning in children. Ava is swept along with them, a leaf in the tidal undertow. There are too many. Some of them are touching her. Infectious. Ava catches the eye of the teacher, who gives her a knowing smile. What is there to smile about? Ava is floundering. Her hand on the hilt. One swipe would give her breathing room. Why is it so hard to be good?

'Come along, children,' calls the teacher, the stragglers trotting to catch up. 'Stay together now.'

And the current passes …

… although the rain has increased. At the top of the hill a bus idles opposite the Savoy cinema. The bus's door is open and Ava seizes the chance. She jumps aboard and sits in the first empty seat. The schoolchildren have moved mercilessly towards the railway station, running through the squall to the shelter of the next shop awning, their voices gradually fading. It's warm in the bus. It smells of hamburgers.

'You got a ticket, love?' asks the driver.

'I don't need a ticket.'

'No ticket, no ride,' he says. He's seen her around town, this old trouble-maker; the other drivers all talk about her. Is she an old trouble-maker? Is that how they see her? Does he wonder how difficult it will be to get her off the bus? She's cadged free rides like this before, not going anywhere, just a round trip back to where she began, and management don't like it, eating into their profit margin. It's the futility of it they don't like. There have been lectures back at the depot. More than his job's worth.

'You're not going anywhere.' Ava is not above stating the obvious. She knows how the system works.

'I have to return to the depot.'

'When?'

'In a few minutes.'

'Then in a few minutes I'll alight. Surely I don't need a ticket to sit here out of the rain. Excuse me while I compose myself.'

With that Ava closes her eyes and sleeps. Or at least gives the correct impression of sleeping. She needs a moment to recover from her conniption. The children fade from her. They've gone. Calm. For a while the sound of rain types on the roof of the bus. She imagines the bus driver's sigh. He knows it's not worth causing a fuss, and she's right, he's not going anywhere. Management can like it or lump it. How would it look? Kicking an old lady off his bus in the rain. Others would, he knows. Bus driving and being a stickler for the rules are surely not the only things in his life – although what else there may be is not immediately clear to Ava with her eyes clamped shut.

A couple of other passengers poke their heads into the bus and enquire about the trip to Medlow Bath. The bus driver beckons them on board but, seeing Ava slumped in the front seat, mouth agape, thighs agape, they hover between bus and shelter on the footpath, muttering to themselves.

'Hey, lady,' says the bus driver.

Ava snorts. A grampus.

'Hey. You're scaring my passengers.'

'I thought you had to go back to the depot,' says Ava, her eyes firmly closed.

'I do. Eventually. Look, lady, you're going to have to get off unless you buy a ticket.'

Revitalised, at least in principle, Ava rises to her feet. The rain has eased. The schoolchildren have gone. She's sure they're not intentionally evil, it's just the impression they give.

'You are a naughty bus driver,' she says, stepping down. 'I know the likes of you. Your sort. No more bullshit.'

And approaching the wary passengers on the footpath, wagging her finger, she repeats:

'No more bullshit.'

AFTERNOON

AFTERNOON

IT MUST BE THE SMELL of hamburgers that reminds Ava she is hungry. Where can she get a feed at a time like this? If the librarians will not stump her up a sambo then she is pretty sure the next-door council-run soup kitchen for pensioners and old folk will. It's quite the community service. Not that she considers herself a pensioner or an old person, but one seeks advantage where one finds it. Not so? So. She is a chameleon. Adapt and survive. She wonders if they serve hermaphrodites. However, the prospect of having that conversation again is exhausting. All she wants is some tucker. She marches on. March or fall, as they say in the Foreign Legion. Darwinian. Do they still say that? she wonders. If they don't then they ought to. Sort the sheep from the cacti. Beau Geste, he was the fellow. A manly man. Ava thinks about the Foreign Legionnaires she has known and loved. The way they *strut*, heading off into the desert with a carbine over their shoulders. Ava envies a man his capacity to strut.

She struts back down the hill, retracing her steps. The soup kitchen is located in the hall off the square next door to the treacherous library. Pigeons congregate on the courtyard flagstones outside. She is half tempted to go into the library and make a nuisance of herself again, ask for a copy of *Beau Geste*, the 1923 edition, talk the hind leg off a cooking pot till they get that glazed-over look in their eyes. However, she has learned her lesson, if not the error of her ways. Vandalism is all very well, but you'd really rather want it to be for something more meaningful than the latest bestseller. Plus she had had to pay for the book.

Scattering the pigeons, she wipes her feet on the mat. There, that's responsible; that's community-spirited. She pushes open the door and enters the hall. There are a dozen old people mumbling over their sandwiches and cups of coffee. Some are playing cards. Others knitting. A few look up at her entrance. At least it's warm, and it smells nice. She takes off her helmet and hangs it on the hat rack by the door. The other hats on it are all beanies or cloth caps. She joins the queue. She thinks calm thoughts. The man in front of her turns and embarks on a conversation with himself seemingly for her edification.

'Keeping out of the weather? That's the spirit. Lovely day earlier. I saw a currawong carrying a pine cone, would you believe it? I hope it's stroganoff today, they do a grand stroganoff. You like stroganoff?'

He's wearing a vest the colour of stroganoff, so perhaps that's where the connection comes from. He has a nose to be proud of, like a turnip gone to seed. Ava sizes up the strength of his hand and declines to shake it. Strogawhat?

The queue moves forward and people take their plates of food and disperse. In a while she is being asked another question. It's slightly alarming to be asked a question so directly by a stranger. It's the sort of question one might ask of God, if the opportunity arose. She has to check the palpitations in her spleen for symptoms, but there are none. God is silent. Again the question from a friendly-faced man wearing a paper hat: 'What would you like?'

Ava prevaricates. There is an issue of pride here.

'What would I like? What would I like? Some soup, please. If that's at all possible. If I can't have world peace, then some soup.'

'Sure,' says the man, who does not, Ava knows, care a fig for world peace or whether literature exists, ladling up a generous splash into a china bowl, a creeping vine of bluebells about the rim. A bread roll to boot.

'Butter?'

'*Merci.*'

'There you go.'

He wipes a slice of butter onto the side plate with her roll.

'Thank you.'

It's such a simple gift. And no questions asked, apart from the practical ones. Nothing too abstract or philosophical. *What would she like?* If not world peace, then how about a gun? A gun for everyone. Her stomach rumbles impatiently. She wonders how many lunches has she had in her life? That would require some complicated arithmetic. Do bees stop for lunch, or do they eat on the wing? There's a question. If you told them to stop working so hard, would they?

Ava takes her soup and finds a seat at a table away from the old crustaceans and their complex desperation, amongst which is a need to avenge themselves on the world, or perhaps their own younger selves. Some of them stare at her. She takes off her coat and hangs it on the back of the chair. Her bag on the table. She smooths her grey hair. Where is her helmet? It's over there on the hat rack. She'll forget her head one of these … The steam from the soup and her salivary glands combine to do their business. She blows on it like a man practising how to whistle. It is just the right temperature. There are vegetables. And bits of chicken. She dunks her bread roll into it and sucks the limp crust with an energetic purpose that she did not, until that moment, know was in her. She sucks it like she's sucking the entrails from a sparrow flung down by the hand of God. She feels the equation bubbling in her belly. Appetite equals life. It's a mathematical law.

Suddenly an impulse strikes her with a laugh and she grabs a couple of paper napkins. Burrowing at the bottom of her bag she finds the stub of a pencil, and her muscles know what to do, her body remembers. Her handwriting is beautiful.

At the end of the crayon road
Sits the memory-fuelled house
Daubed with the old threnode
Of stone monuments and loss.
The centre comes at great cost
Where all thought is aborted.
Ghosts of the past denounce
Their former lives diverted.
Once the house all golden hope
Resided in, now winter's amnesia

Locks it out, and the climber's rope
Linking him to solid earth, that treasure,
Is nothing but a tangle, an imbroglio
Of ambition thwarted by fools.
A storm exhales its jumble
Of clouds that disobey the rules.

At that moment a cold wind blows the door open and she glances up momentarily. A figure walks in and the currents of air in the room seem to slow right down. It is the alien from earlier this morning. Or at least one similar, with a motorcycle helmet and a space suit, or perhaps it is a jacket, the sort they use to keep out the wind. Ava has the eerie feeling that the figure is looking for her. How else can she explain this coincidence? By chance, darling, that's how, she tells herself. God's hiccup. One motorcyclist likes grog; another likes soup. They've as much right to sustenance as anyone else. But then, she considers, not everything revolves around her. The threads of coincidence are a makeshift tapestry. There, that's nice, she thinks. The threads of coincidence. From the edge of her attention she notices the man slowly take off his helmet. Even from this distance she can see he's handsome. A handsome man is a deceptive gift. And yes, he does remind her of the fictitious Engels. She can see he's got an Adam's apple to be proud of, and, while she's aware of what they say about the significance of the Adam's apple, she knows they're not all they're cut out to be.

Nevertheless, she keeps her head down over her napkins, behind a little vase with a plastic daffodil sticking up out of it like a periscope, camouflaging herself amongst the old people—

One of them shouts: 'Snap!'

She's got a lot on her mind and the pencil is helping.

The maelstrom is a code
For losing language, word by word
Imaginings swirl and topple
From the mighty pedestal
Of higher things. It is far to fall
And the gorge is strewn with rocks.
The threads of coincidence
Are makeshift and frail
Ideas lost, large and minuscule,
On the tongue's broken building blocks.

Another word for maelstrom, she thinks, what is it – where you stir the tea too vigorously with a spoon? Nope, it's gone. Perhaps there is no word for it.

She folds the napkins together and stuffs them in the bottom of her bag. Fodder for later.

The tall spaceman gazes about the room but now does not seem to be looking for anything in particular.

Someone shouts: 'Shut the door.'

The figure pulls the helmet on again, eyeless behind the visor, and backs out, hand raised in apology. The draught goes with him and the air stills. So, others could see it too, Ava thinks. It's not just me. She is not even the centre of her own imaginings. She's at the periphery of her delusions. And from the edge of her dark mind she can hear the sound of hooves, or is it glass breaking? She smells the daffodil, even though she knows it is plastic.

She quickly gobbles down the rest of the bread roll. The fragrant steam wants to make her blow her nose. Perhaps she's coming down with something? Cancer, maybe. Here in public she does not elect to employ the bushman's hankie. Instead she reaches into a pocket and discovers not her kerchief but a withered apricot. How did that get there? For a second she thinks it might be an organ which has somehow slipped through a hole from her stomach into her pocket. In another pocket she finds a green fig. In another, ah, some toilet paper. She blows her nose with a wipe and a wiggle, leaving the sodden tissues in the ash tray. She gives full focus to the remains of the soup, lukewarm now, chewing the cud of a well-cooked carrot. Nothing like a well-cooked carrot. Glancing up at the clock she sees that already it is afternoon.

* * *

Where has the day gone? What has she accomplished? If only she had another life. She fortifies herself with a surreptitious swig from the sherry bottle, slides it back into her overcoat pocket. Mr Stroganoff watches her from his own table nearby, still talking to himself. She does not catch his eye for fear he may try to engage her in further conversation. What must it be like living inside his head? That's the trouble with these poor old blabbermouths; they think their opinions are the most important you're going to come across in a day's march and you can never get a word in edgeways. Well, stuff and pickle that for a joke. Coat on, helmet on, bag over her shoulder, Ava leaves the warm, steamy hall and steps outdoors again. Again the pigeons erupt upwards, settling on the low-hanging eaves of the library, place of betrayal and deceit. For a moment she wonders what pigeon tastes like. One of these days, you never know, maybe it might come to that. She heads uphill towards the railway station and the underpass. It might be interesting to enumerate her steps, she thinks, count how many steps to the corner, but that would be pathological, like wanting to know how many lunches she's had, and Ava is not pathological, no matter what they say. To mention the word stroganoff three times in the one breath, now that's pathological. She is lucid and aware, on the verge of a new discovery. She just needs to clarify what it is without falling into the lava again. How would you begin to imagine, for example, your way into another person's shoes when your own are so riddled with holes?

* * *

From the edge of her imaginings Ava can see Mitch coming, as if on a horse, galloping towards her ...

Mitchell Dunning (they call him Mitch although sometimes they call him Dunny) has been sent by his boss to fetch four hot pies and a litre of chocolate milk from the bottom bakery in Katoomba Street. His boss has tossed him the keys and a twenty-dollar note with specific instructions. Sauce on his. And don't drag the chain. Dunny can have what he likes. Ava sees them as clearly as if they were on a piece of pink paper, busy chopping down a big tree, a *Pinus radiata*, growing too close to the railway line along Bathurst Road. Mitchell works for Gary Bailey, whose business goes by the fanciful title of Bailey's Tree Surgery. *Pruning. Removal. Chipping. Free quotes.*

Mitchell is nineteen. Ava remembers nineteen.

It is Bailey's job to monkey up the trees with the assistance of two great spikes embedded in his boots, which stick into the sides of the trunks as if he is climbing a glacier. A noble, manly pursuit. Starting at the top he cuts the uppermost branches with a small chainsaw which dangles from a hefty leather belt at his waist. He leans into the safety harness like a leather pelvis, the belt which wraps around the tree somehow keeping him up there in defiance of gravity. (Can you imagine it? In defiance of gravity!) The size of the chainsaw increases the lower down the tree he comes, so that when he is at last on the ground it is a monster-sized chainsaw that slices up the trunk like a wheel of cheese. Mitchell spends a lot of time with his head craned back watching for hand signals as to what he is supposed to do. Fetch. Carry. Look out. It is his job to gather up and collect these lighter branches, the brush, as they float down (it is a deceptive illusion), and stack them into piles where they can be cut into a more manageable size before being carted off or chipped into garden mulch. As a young man Dunny is impressed with all this destruction that he wants so much to be part of. His job involves a lot of sweat and a stiff neck. He is still young enough to take his body for granted. That morning, once the tree is down, Bailey says to Mitchell: 'Here's twenty bucks. Take my ute and go fetch us four pies from the bakery and don't be all day about it. And don't forget the sauce.'

Bailey has no sons, but he has five daughters. Why not? Ava's imagination is going off at a tangent, but never mind. Mitchell finds it amusing that Bailey has, through force of propinquity, come to adopt their style of speaking. Huh? Wiry, gristly, middle-aged Bailey often uses the language of his teenage daughters quite unconsciously to engage with people, and to express his more general disdain of the world. He regularly calls Mitchell a *dweeb*, or a *nerd*, or a *goose*, or a *dropkick*, or a *total*. He says *oh man*, and *wow*, more often than necessary, and *calm the farm*, and *take a chill pill*, language which seems completely out of place in his sun-creased mouth. He dislikes Mitchell simply because he is of an age his daughters might possibly find interesting. They do not. At least, ostensibly. They refer to their father's labourer, who turns up early each morning while they breakfast in their pyjamas, as that dweeb, nerd, goose or dropkick, and ask him embarrassing questions like *What sort of cheese do you eat?*

Ava sees that question in quotation marks. She does not know the answer.

They ridicule the sparseness of his beard. However, they do it with passion. Bailey therefore makes Mitchell work harder than he might another groundsman of another age. He even makes Mitchell work in the rain, as he might have done a son he was trying to mould in his own image. Mitchell secretly hates Bailey, and he hates the daughters also, for all their skimpy breakfast pyjamas and the way they scratch themselves unselfconsciously. He doesn't even like cheese. He hopes Bailey's safety harness might one day snap, with all the heroics that would entail. Mitch wishes instead that he had been sent to the café where Marjorie works. He likes her, but no, Bailey wants pies.

So Mitchell takes the keys and the twenty dollars and climbs into Bailey's ute. He is exhausted, and sitting down, even like this for five minutes, feels slightly luxurious. Being paid to sit down, is that a perk of the adult world? Being paid to drive to the shops. It is almost decadent. He is prepared to enjoy this brief respite from the hard physical labour of the morning. The cuffs of his pants are full of sawdust which spills on the floor of the ute. He intends to take his time and feel the breeze. He turns the radio on. The radio plays 'Bennie and the Jets'. He drives into town and finds a spot to park in the main street. For a brief moment, behind the wheel, he can pretend he is Mr Bailey, *Tree Surgeon*. He can imagine he has another life.

The girl in the bakery has just the sort of hair Mitch likes, though not as honey-blond as Marjorie's. She is glowing from the heat of the ovens, and the smell of baking he attributes to her. There is cinnamon in the air. He makes his order and she packs four pies into paper bags for him.

'Sauce?'

'Yeah. Better. Not on mine. Thanks.'

'Bye, Dunny.'

Not knowing how to talk to her he pockets the change, Bailey is sure to count it, and steps outside. There was a squall before, but it looks like the rain is passing. Mindful of

Bailey's order not to dawdle – he's been long enough – Mitch presses his foot down on the accelerator, climbing as fast as the ute will go up the steep hill towards the corner. And now he is coming.

* * *

Ava goes into the Paragon café and asks for a spare plastic bag. They look at her curiously, it is after all a chocolate shop, not a plastic bag shop; however, they give her one, proving that not all human interaction is fraught with self-interest. She wraps her new ream of paper in the plastic and secures it in her calico sack, which is secreted now beneath her coat, giving her an odd, lumpy shape. Just in case the rain ... She's thinking ahead. There is a woman on the footpath collecting signatures, or money, or both from passersby. She's calling out to people – *save* something, or *free* something, or *stop* something, it's not clear what. Her protest sign would take some dedicated reading, there's such a lot of fine print on it. She's just the sort Ava would often stop and chew the fat with. Save what? Free what? Do they want to be saved? Normally she would stop and engage with the finer points of the fine print. Spelling, for example. Syntax. The meaning of apocalypse. But today she doesn't.

She continues up the hill to the corner, soup still warm in her belly. Cars swishing up and down the street. People filing into the Savoy to see the lunchtime feature, which today is a family show called *Death Wish* starring Charles Bronson. Two hundred and forty-three steps from the Paragon to the corner. She steps off the footpath between two parked cars. Another vehicle, a ute, nips around the curve of the corner – appears slowly out of nowhere – skidding suddenly on the wet road, and, Ava looming large, knocks her flying into the gutter. Does the sound of breaking glass come before the impact, or after? She sees herself flying, putting out her hands to break her fall. The road rising to meet her. It's like she's already bounced back up again, but she hasn't.

Then there's an awful thump and pies go tumbling off the seat. In her pocket the sherry bottle bursts dully, muffled by toilet paper and figs, and the left-hand headlight of the ute bursts on impact with the bottle. The wind is knocked from her sails. Her head cracks on the road, lucky she's wearing her ... Ava is surprised to find herself lying in the gutter looking at the stars. Who said that? No, no stars. Clouds. Lying in the gutter looking at the clouds. Not even clouds, just a grey, overhanging canopy of cumulo— of cumulo— of fog. Or is that her eyes glazing over? Street signs and shop awnings. Little pinpricks of drizzle needling her face.

'Oh fuck,' she says.

The sky seems to grow purple over her. Christ, her leg hurts. In a moment there are people, men mostly, filling her view with their broad shoulders. The expressions on their faces all wide-eyed with concern, all talking at once.

'Are you all right?' asks one.

'Is she dead?' asks another.

'Where does it hurt?'

'Can you get up?'

'Don't try to move.'

Too many imperatives.

'No, I'm not dead,' she answers the most important question first. Surely that much is obvious? She can feel the rainwater in the gutter seeping through her beautiful pinstriped trousers. It's not warm like blood, so that's a positive sign. Her helmet she sees lying further along the street, the carmine velvet of its interior upturned like a Pope's begging bowl. She tries to sit up, but someone holds her down. Her hand finds a numb lump on her head somewhere between the size of a wren's egg and an emu's egg.

'Best not to move, I think.'

'I'm all right,' she says, although her thigh hurts, not so much from the impact, but from the damned broken bottle. All these friends, worried for her welfare. It's a surprise that so many people care for her. Better not let that feeling go too soon. In adversity breeds friendship. These dozens, scores, hundreds of friends, all concerned about her. There was that lady at the fence. She was nice. What was her name again? Marjorie from the coffee shop, the chap who gave her soup, all with a kind word, a human face. Would you class that as friendship? Are they friendships worth dying for, like the one Dave had with Red? The lost love of sisterhood. Time immemorial. Two hundred and forty-three steps.

Mitchell appears in the throng, looking down at her, shaken, nervously tugging the wisps of his beard.

'Is he all okay? He just stepped out in front of me.'

'It's a lady.'

'Someone call an ambulance.'

'A lady? I thought it was a man. Just stepped out in front of me. I wasn't speeding.'

Ava manages to sit up.

'Get off me,' she says to the owner of the hands holding her down.

'Better not move, love,' says another fellow.

'I'm fine. But you really ought to watch where you're driving, young man.'

'I'm sorry,' says Mitchell.

Ava studies his face, trying to decipher his shock, but that would appear to be impossible.

'It wasn't your fault, son,' says someone else.

Where the sherry bottle has broken, Ava can feel her pocket full of glass like seashells or shark teeth. That's what is hurting her, the glass cutting through her trousers into her thigh; that and the humiliation.

'Here's a cop,' says someone else.

Pushing his way through the curious crowd – Ava recognises the young policeman from earlier this morning.

'You again,' he says, giving her the once-over.

'Well, if it isn't Officer Tickle-my-toes,' she says, grimacing.

'Are you hurt?'

'Tickety-boo,' says Ava, 'except for my leg.'

'She just stepped out in front of me,' says Mitchell, looking around for some support.

'I think she's been drinking,' says another stickybeak.

Everyone trying to get in on the drama.

'Let me up,' says Ava again.

It is hard to retain a skerrick of dignity while sitting in the gutter surrounded by inquisitive well-wishers.

'She must be drunk.'

And some not-so-well. Passersby staring from the foot-path. The traffic banking up behind the ute with one broken headlight, like a doll with one eye.

'Can you move your leg?'

'I think so.'

Her hip is starting to hurt now, but she thinks she'll keep that information to herself.

'Here's the ambulance,' says another voice, and with the utterance of that phrase all her problems have been solved—

Or else they're just starting. The ambulance pulls up along-side the kerb, blocking the other side of the road. That's more like it: bring the city to a standstill, she thinks. Cool as a couple of Siamese cats the ambulance men step from the vehicle, its light twirling lazily on the roof. With their arrival the histrionics subside and the onlookers start to move away, going about their business. No one will be asked to block a spurting artery with a thumb; no one is going to need to hold a limb while it is amputated here at the roadside. Save that story for the dinner table.

The ambulance men give Ava a cursory examination. They peer into her eyes, feel her head – *ouch* – watch it, fellah. They check her pulse and other vital signs. They ask her questions, one of which is: 'Did you hit your head?'

'No.'

'How did you get this lump?'

'Oh, all right then.'

They find the broken glass in her pocket, mixed up with some walnut shells and lacerated green figs.

'I'm all right, I tell you.'

116

They decide (Ahmed and Ben) that to be on the safe side they'll take her to the hospital for observation and some precautionary X-rays. This news releases a squirt of adrenaline in Ava.

'Not the hospital. I can't go to the hospital.'

She swoons against Officer Fowler's arm.

'It's a precaution.'

'I hate the hospital.'

'I'm afraid it's protocol,' says one of the ambulance men, Ben, 'when someone hits their head.'

'But I'm fine, really I'm fine. See, I can stand. I can walk a straight line. Besides, I'm needed at home.'

'We'll be the judge of that,' says the other, Ahmed, a nice-looking boy with a pair of red-roseleaf lips. If only they'd let the nice ones talk to her. Officer Fowler waves the remaining onlookers away, nothing to see here. Despite her protestations they gently manoeuvre her to the back of the ambulance, checking how she favours one leg. At least it's not broken.

'How's your hip, love?'

'Fine. How's yours?'

'Fine.'

'I won't go to the hospital,' she says, 'I can't.'

'Too late.'

They hoist her up the step into the rear of the vehicle. Ava feels like she is mounting a catafalque, though without the ceremony. She looks out at the dissipating throng, letting the afternoon return and settle after having been blown about by the commotion like leaves, or like a new perm on a windy day.

'Just stepped out in front of me,' Mitchell is saying to Fowler on the footpath. Ava can read their body language like a Saturday pantomime.

'How fast were you going?'

'Not fast.'

'How fast, exactly?'

The townsfolk return to their interrupted business. In her café Marjorie, busy with the lunchtime rush, must be wondering why the traffic has backed up past the window and down the hill.

The drama moves on. Much as Ava likes to be the centre of attention she does not like to be the cause of a commotion, unless it is a literary one over her opinion on the latest best-seller, say. However, at the moment that is not important.

'Please, please don't—'

But they do. They close the doors and she is trapped like a sparrow inside a mausoleum. Immediately she wants to go to the toilet. The driver, Ahmed, goes round to the driver's seat and starts the engine. She weighs up her options, breathing rapidly. Going with the flow seems to be the most sensible course at the moment. Resistance, as they say, is useless. She does not tell them, for instance, that the hospital is located on the way home to her hut (she passed it this morning, remember) so this is cheaper than a taxi. They're doing her a favour. It will save her some shoe leather when she is ready to make her escape. They don't need to know her ulterior motives. She hopes the young driver won't have to go to gaol for his part in the misadventure. He probably needs someone to take him aside and give him a pat on the back. Would nice

Officer Fowler have that in him? she wonders. She lies back and lets the ambulance medic examine her, laying his cold fingers on her skin like a soothsayer at the ouija board.

His cursory field study has already uncovered the machete beneath the coat.

'What's this for?'

'Dogs.'

'What dogs?'

'All dogs. It's very useful.'

He accepts this. He's been around. Seen everything. He can see she's nervous. Helping her into the ambulance he sensed her resistance. Some people hate hospitals, it's true.

'My hat,' she squawks, but she's not wearing a hat. She's like a stubborn cat on a flywire screen that will not be moved. She wilts. Should she scream? She's one step from death, lying there on the bench. Her hat gone. Ben, in the back with her, asks her how she feels and she replies:

'Short of breath. Dizzy. Peripatetic.'

She asks for some oxygen just so she can hear the hiss of the cylinder. Ben obliges.

'What's this for?' she asks, reaching out for something silver and shiny.

'Don't touch that.' He slaps her hand softly. Tut tut. 'It's been an all right day, hasn't it? Apart from the rain.'

He's trying to keep her talking, to distract her, but Ava feels more tired than in pain.

'A great day,' she says, dissembling. She rubs her shoulder. He holds the mask to her face and Ava breathes in the smell of rubber and metal. Ahmed, the driver, turns a couple of corners. Too soon they are at the hospital – it really is only down the road a way – idling up the Emergency ramp. Hardly worth the effort. They didn't even have to turn the siren on.

The rear doors are opened by an Emergency nurse. Ahmed and Ben help Ava down to a waiting wheelchair.

'Thanks very much,' she says, putting on a brave face, 'I can walk from here.'

'No you don't,' says the nurse, placing a restraining hand on her shoulder, easing her with some authority into the chair. The automatic doors glide open and the nurse wheels her through. When the door shuts behind them again, Ava feels immediately breathless, like the air has been sucked out of the building and she's breathing cement dust. She doesn't want to share the air. There's only enough for her. The Emergency department opens out before them. At the same time this desperate urge to micturate – right now – comes over her again. If she doesn't she'll burst, here all over the floor. But the urge is distracted (what urge?) by another nurse, who appears like an archangel with a clipboard, asking her name. What to answer? Ava or Oscar, or something else? There are so many choices.

'Oscar,' says Ava. Oscar will come to her rescue.

'Really? Oscar.'

'Indeed.'

She pursues the matter of the surname, which takes a little clarification.

'I have a certificate of deed poll somewhere here.'

She ferrets about in her bag.

'Never mind,' says the nurse, 'I believe you.'

This exchange is followed by the query: 'Address?'

'Olympus.'

The nurse writes that down, thinking it might be a street name. She no doubt has her own problems which Ava can't begin to imagine at the moment, although if she put her mind to it …

'Am I under arrest?' Oscar asks.

'No. Of course not.'

'Am I then free to go?'

'Well, yes, but we want to make sure nothing's broken.'

'As in?'

'As in bones.'

'I see.'

'Let's go in here.'

She wheels Ava into a cubicle and whips a rattling curtain about them to form a Bedouin's tent.

'This is cosy,' says Ava.

'What happened?' The nurse asks this of the ambulance medic, Ben, who is loitering in the background waiting for a tip like an attendant at the entombment of a pharaoh, the one who extricates the brains piece by piece with a spatula and puts them in a ceramic jar.

'Pedestrian hit by MV. Minor lacerations to right thigh. Also arrhythmia.'

The nurse nods, writes this down.

'Don't forget my scybalum,' says Ava.

Ben, his duty done, goes away, far away, to his own narrative beyond the doors. It is impossible for her to keep track of them all.

'Where does it hurt, dear?' The nurse turns back to Ava. She must have a name too. A whole history behind those green eyes.

'My duodenum,' Ava answers. This makes the nurse open and shut her mouth a few times.

'Anywhere else?'

'My throat is a limekiln, my brain a furnace, and my nerves a coil of angry adders.'

'That sounds serious. How about we make sure your leg's not fractured for starters. Do you want to put your bag on this chair?'

'No.'

There are a few further questions which Ava cannot remember and to which she lets Oscar make up the responses.

'Are you allergic to penicillin?'

'I have the simplest tastes. I am always satisfied with the best.'

The nurse (Susan: it's on the ID tag hanging from a little chain about her ivory neck), who has had a busy morning, casts Ava aside to wait, for how long she does not know, and in that time Ava manages to close her eyes, which is pleasant. It's nice here in this tent. She listens to the hustle and bustle of medical emergencies going on about her. It's like a radio serial. In a while the nurse returns and continues with her esoteric procedure, filling in a few more forms.

'Now let's have a look at this leg.'

Ava unclasps her braces and stands to lower her strides. The machete handle clatters on the floor (the blade is still in its sheath). Susan does not even glance at it. She puts her face to the gash on Ava's white thigh. There is a loose triangle of skin flapping and a strawberry slick of blood descending her leg, drying around the edges.

'Nasty. What caused that?'

'Figs.'

'Figs?'

'Yes.'

'It might need a stitch or two. We'll get doctor to take a look.'

'Bugger doctor,' says Ava, and the nurse laughs. Human at least, they agree on something. Nurse makes a few phone calls. Ava wonders if she is calling the wardens, if she is being sectioned again.

Her bladder burns. In a while a young doctor appears, whisking the flap of the tent aside. He has sleepless eyes and eyebrows that almost join together. Ava can see the pores in his nose. He perfunctorily examines Ava's leg.

'Nasty. What caused that?'

'Time's winged chariot.'

'I thought you said figs,' says Nurse Susan.

Ava shrugs.

'Right,' says the doctor. 'Well, it'll need a few stitches. Can you clean her up, please, nurse?'

'Yes, doctor.'

Ava cannot stand the hierarchy of the place, the condescension. The doctor steps out of the tent while Susan swabs Ava's leg with moist cotton-wool balls. *Ouch.* The water in the little bowl turns pink. The doctor returns with an upright hypodermic syringe. He jabs it into Ava's thigh – *Ouch! Fuck! Ouch!* – just above the hypotenuse that still joins the flap of skin to the rest of her.

'Did that hurt?'

'Of course it bloody hurt.'

'It's just a local. You won't feel anything in a moment.'

And he's right. The anaesthetic quickly starts to work. She can't tell if the wound has been caused by glass from the broken headlight or glass from the sherry bottle. What a tragic waste. Ava watches the doctor as he sews six evenly spaced sutures, three along each open side of the triangle. She can feel the pressure of the needle as it pierces her skin, the tension of the thread drawing through, but no pain, thank goodness. She leans nearer the doctor. She's close enough to see the beginnings of tomorrow's whiskers. She wonders what would happen if she bit his ear?

'That should knit together nicely,' says the doctor, packing away his sewing kit. 'You'll have a little war wound to boast about.'

'What doesn't kill me makes me stronger,' says Ava.

'Something like that.'

The doctor glances at her as if suddenly aware that she is a person. She smiles sweetly. He exits the Bedouin tent leaving the curtain wide open. Nurse Susan swabs the war wound with some antiseptic and places a bandage over it. What is all the fuss about? Ava wonders.

Ava glances around at the Emergency ward. The silver stands – hat racks, are they? A man on crutches. A woman with her arm in a sling. When they look at her through the door of the tent, absorbed in the tall story of their own crisis, she becomes nothing but a bare-legged woman on a gurney. One of the broken. Is that her only story? You are no more than your disease. Well, that's a lot of horse shit, thinks Ava. It's barely a scratch. Now's the time to get out of here; she has been co-operative long enough. Susan opens up the sides of the tent. Lying on a nearby stretcher is another fellow with a white patch over one eye, waiting patiently for the eagle to return and peck out the other. Hospitals are places of poisoned memory for Ava, not recovery. She slides off the bed and picks up her trousers, with the machete swinging loosely.

'Let's leave this here, shall we?'

'Why?'

'It'll make the machine go berserk.'

'What do you mean? I want to leave.'

'Not yet, dear. There's a few more tests to be done.'

It's all too much. Ava slumps back into the wheelchair. Without her helmet she's like jelly.

'If you must,' she says, resigned. *'I suppose I shall have to die beyond my means.'*

Soon, she knows, the eagle will come for her.

'No one's going to die,' says Nurse Susan, presumptuously, as if she knows something more than she's letting on.

The nurse places the machete on a nearby chair.

'It must be returned to me untarnished and unscathed,' says Ava. 'In fact I would like a surety.'

'We don't do sureties.'

'What sort of outfit are you running here?'

'Let's get you X-rayed, then we'll see. How are you feeling?'

'Not ill,' says Oscar, *'but very weary.'*

'Let's leave your pants here too. What lovely material.'

125

'Thank you. We like them a lot.'

Susan fingers the cloth as if it is cash. 'I love your … what is that? A cravat?'

'Indeed. And I love your bib,' replies Ava. 'Isn't this a lovely little chat we're having about fashion.'

The nurse doesn't appreciate Ava's tone.

'You can pop this gown on, please.'

Against her instincts Ava struggles into the gown, open and breezy at the back. She only does it because Susan is being so nice to her.

'What's this on your stomach?' the nurse asks.

'I don't know.'

'It looks like ink.'

'My stock-in-trade,' says Ava, wrapping the gown around her.

'Good. And here, take these.'

She gives Ava three pills, which Ava knocks back without water.

'I actually meant for later. It'll throb when that local wears off. Here, these are for tonight.'

Susan hands Ava some more pills in an alfoil sachet, which she hides in the breast pocket of her linen shirt. Thankfully it has remained relatively untarnished through this ordeal.

'Tell me, when did you last eat?'

'I've just had lunch,' says Ava, 'thank you.'

'What did you eat?'

'Soup.'

'And is there anyone at home for you?'

'Oh yes.'

'That's good.'

'Yes, Plutus and Bacchus.'

Nurse Susan gives this information a moment's digestion, then shrugs to herself.

She wheels Ava off in the chair down a squeaky-clean corridor. Lights reflect in it like Chinese lanterns in the Yangtze. They turn a corner. Another. They're getting further and further from the exit. It's a rat maze.

'I need to micturate,' says Ava.

'Really? Can't you wait till after the X-ray?'

'No.'

Nurse Susan, with pretty wisps of hair floating from under her cap like shreds of spider web, takes a detour to the lavatory – and there are the two doors again, the eternal question. The dark fellow with the sickle and cowl. Homme or Femme? Ava's dilemma returns. It never really goes away; it just resurfaces now and then in times of crisis, like the oil and jetsam fired from a torpedo tube masquerading as death.

'I can walk,' says Ava.

'That's good. Not broken then.'

Ava stands. Her leg throbs but she can stand alone. A statue. A mountain. All praise to the vertical. Quick as a ferret she darts into the male toilet. The nurse calls out:

'Oscar, that's the wrong door.'

But Ava is already through. Too late, sister. Homme. There is no one within and she locks herself into a cubicle. She breathes. Calm. Hardly claustrophobic at all. She opens the gown and examines her thigh. Just a scratch underneath the bandage. It's a nice job. The bruise, she knows, will come up later, but bruises are signs of adversity and triumph. What she has had to struggle through for her art. It's quiet here and she takes her time. The relief is like all her troubles being lifted at once, but there is never a total respite from trouble. That's what being human is.

Echo of her breathing. She rests her forehead against the cold white wall of the cubicle. How did she get here? To this point? She wishes she had taken better care of her topi. She feels desperately weary, wonders if it might be opportune to take a little nap …

There is a tap at the door and she starts awake. How long has she been asleep?

'Are you all right, dear?'

The nurse is waiting with the chair, ready to humour her. You naughty little patient, her frown says, but she holds her tongue. Ava pulls up her underpants, flushes, then sits back down in the chair.

'I was dreaming of the Cotswolds.'

'Really?'

'No, but I've always wanted to say that, dreaming of the Cotswolds. Drive on,' she says.

Along the corridors there are pictures, old photographs of doctors and high-faluting administrators, scowling down as if scowling down was some sort of heritage. One of them is a dour fellow with a fine moustache, looking off into the distance. What she would give to be able to grow a moustache like that. Susan wheels her on to the X-ray clinic. A door to an inner sanctum. She hands over Ava's chart to two other nurses. A technician lurks behind a thickened glass window. They examine her chart on its little masonite clipboard. At the top it says in important-looking letters: *Western Area Health*. Suddenly Ava is the sort of person who has a chart. She remembers what power they hold and what use they can be put to. Tool of the oppressor, the chart will be satisfied. The nurses manoeuvre her into the annexe with the expensive equipment. It's like being in the bowels of a submarine, her torpedo tubes full of oil and detritus. One of the new nurses has powerful wrists like a man. Ava gives her a quick second glance: nope, she's a woman. Through the window the technician looks at the instruments and dials.

There is a grim, silver table on which they expect her to lie. It is like the slab in an abattoir. The nurses barely blink at the big white male underpants exposed at the back of the gown. Unexpectedly she whimpers.

'Listen, Oscar,' says Susan kindly, 'we need to make sure your leg isn't fractured, so we're going to sit you up here and take a photograph.'

'I can walk, can't I?'

'It's a routine procedure. It won't hurt,' says the one with the thick wrists.

'That's what you all say,' says Ava, but without her machete, without her coat, or helmet, she feels defenceless. She has been reduced. She is a patient with a chart and her brain in a jar. She cannot resist. They are relentless. Oscar fades away towards the back of the room, a little boy crouching in the corner, everyone laughing at him.

'If you must,' she says.

They manage to get her on the table. *Ouch* and *ooh* and *aah*.

'Lift your bottom, dear.'

She does, and they slide the zinc plate or whatever it is under her leg. It's cold. They position the camera overhead, a red cross shining on the target of her thigh.

'Now lie still.'

They go behind the lead screen and peer at her through the window. Ava lies still as a dead kangaroo in the grass at the side of the road. Let all the rot that hides in her keep still and silent; let no one sniff her out. She tries to think of nothing. She hears the machines click and whirr. The nurses come back in and roll her into another position, manipulating her like a sausage.

'Comfy, dear?'

'I'm cold.'

'It won't take long.'

The process is repeated. They take a few more snaps. They shift the zinc plate and replace it under her head.

'It says here that you bumped your head.'

They're reading her chart, noses wrinkling at the stench of corruption.

'Not badly,' says Ava, feeling the lump on her noggin.

'Nevertheless, it's protocol.'

That is what makes her feel the worst, the machine with its red light gazing into her mind. She is jelly. Click and whirr. After a while the first nurse returns and rolls her off the table.

'Righto, Oscar, you can get dressed now.'

'My name's Ava,' says Ava softly.

'Is it? It says Oscar on the form, which is a funny sort of name for a woman, although I've seen funnier. I thought it must have been Polish.'

'Polish? No, I was born in Coonabarabran.'

The nurse prefers to believe the form. They busy themselves with the machine and the development of the pictures. Ava dislikes the feel of the air on her legs. She knows she has to get out of here before the photos are developed and her secrets are revealed and they keep her here forever.

She sits back in the wheelchair, but no one comes for her. She stares at the antiseptic colour scheme on the walls. A kind of wan lavender.

'One of us has got to go,' she says to herself.

Peering through the window she sees the nurses' heads together behind the screen with the technician examining the negatives, writing their judgements on the chart. Perhaps they are laughing at her bones. Ava casually wheels herself around the table to the door.

'Just wait outside for me, dear,' the nurse calls, poking her head around the partition. 'We need to do a few more tests. Then we'll see about organising a bed for you.'

'A bed?' Ava's voice squeaks in a moment of panic.

'Yes, you're malnourished, dear. It's protocol.'

Ava struggles to open the door. She has to wrestle with the pneumatic cushion, but manages to wheel herself out into the hallway. The chair also is an awkward machine. Between them both it is like trying to put on a shirt under water. However, once she's outside and the door sighs shut she jumps up and scampers off down the corridor to the first corner. She glances back. No one's after her. Left, right, left again. Her leg feels good. Hearing voices in the distance she ducks into an office, door unlocked, and waits until they pass, her eye at the crack. The farcical thing would be to have the approaching voices follow her into the office for a tryst or a confabulation or a what-have-you, and Ava ducking under the desk having to endure the clunky love-making overhead. Oh, the comic possibilities. Her mind toys briefly with that idea, but it does not happen. The voices pass. Her heart is racing, surely the excitement of the chase.

'Can I help you?'

Ava spins around to see a man, a doctor by the looks of the white coat, sitting at a desk, a wry expression on his dial. She didn't see him at first, the devil incarnate, surrounded by paperwork.

'And you are?' he asks.

'Dr Langdon,' she says, introducing herself. 'Western Area Health. Splendid job you're doing. Particularly in obstetrics. Keep up the good work. Sorry to interrupt.'

'Are you looking for someone?'

'Dr Wilde, I think is the name.'

'I don't know him.'

'Oh dear. Wasted trip then.'

She ducks back out the door, pulling it behind her, and runs as best she is able down the corridor, passing other offices and clinics. The doctor, she imagines, jumps up and follows her to the door, but she's disappeared. Which way did she go? She has tricked the devil up to his elbows in bureaucracy. Ava hurries on. She wonders if it is beyond the realm of possibility to come by some morphine. Surely in a place like this, but where would one begin to look? What she needs is a white coat; that would help. It's the archetypal disguise. Then she could just walk into someone's office, or a pharmacy, and demand: *Give me an opiate. It's for an emergency.*

And they would.

And she'd be happy.

Nice little dream. Morphine is all very well, but her greater need is to escape. She still has the other bottle of sherry in her calico bag if only she can find her way back to Emergency.

Find a bed for her! – Lock her up, more likely. Inter her without trial. Strap her down and swab her temples. *Time for your clyster, dear.* She glances down other empty linoleum corridors. Peers around corners. The coast is clear. She makes a semi-run for it to the next corner, her feet slapping at the floor. By now she's quite lost. She almost meets a trolley head on, returning from the wards with empty packets of under-appreciated sandwiches. The orderly stares at her but Ava keeps her face averted.

'Are you lost?'

'No.'

Ava does not stop. Keep moving; the predator targets the hesitant. Around the next corner – it's like Pitt Street – the cleaner with his orbital polisher, buffing the shiny floor to within an inch of its mortal days, the fluorescent light glinting off the surface of it like – the current of the Yangtze has moved on – like the coruscations of the afternoon sun off the beachside shallows, the dead soldiers rolling in the water. Ava slows to a walk, avoiding the machine's wide arc. The cleaner does not even look at her, his head down like a minesweeper in no-man's-land, and then she's off again.

Somehow she finds her way back to Emergency. She slows to a stroll. There's her bag and coat and her trousers and boots just where she left them in the Bedouin tent. She flings the white gown to the floor. Quickly pulls on her trousers and adjusts the braces. *Snap*, that gives her some confidence. She pulls on her boots. The machete has gone. She looks frantically for it, under the seat, under the bed. She looks up, aghast, at the broken and maimed residents of Hades. One of these treacherous, machete-stealing opportunists ... She realises she's drawing attention to herself. She coolly puts the coat on, so what if it stinks, then saunters through the casualty ward. She is Oscar Wilde passing among the ravaged hordes. See Oscar saunter, dispensing perfume from the kerchief at his wrist. Don't panic, she tells herself. Act natural. They'll mistake her for a visitor. The automatic doors wheeze open and no one notices anything out of the ordinary as she passes through.

Outside the rain has stopped, the sky still grey as old feathers. Don't celebrate too soon. She decides to avoid the trap of the highway. That's where they'll be looking for her when the alarm is raised. She walks in the unexpected direction, down quiet Woodlands Road, very sneaky, past the old folks' retirement home and the rugby oval towards the cemetery. It's not far to the gate. Should she enumerate the steps? Christ, no! That's what started all this. Her leg aches, but not so badly. Walking is loosening it up, getting the humours flowing. Wounded in action, Red, just give me a Bible to bite on. Walking is the only thing that warms her. The fact that it's starting to burn is a healing sign. She walks fast at first; however, no one is after her, so she slows down. She's done it. She knows the short cut through the cemetery to the returned soldiers' cricket oval and the back streets of Queens Road. They'll never find her there. Ava does not feel superstitious about cemeteries the way Greeks do. Well, perhaps only a little. As she enters at the driveway gates the air immediately seems a little warmer, but that's probably because her heart is working and she's warming up with all the exertion.

She wanders down the hill past the Anglican section. Every denomination with its own select suburb. The Catholics, Methodists, Jews, Presbyterians, Church of England, Greek Orthodox – all segregated as if they might still do a violence to each other. How come, she wonders, there is no Communist section? Or Rotarian? Slowly it dawns on her that she has to stop. The blood in her temples pounds savagely. Deciding to give her leg a rest she slows, and finds a suitable gravestone on which to catch her breath. Here's a clean, fresh one. Theodore Albert Whitaker. It's just like visiting him in hospital. Poor old Theodore, just let him sleep. Who were you, old sport? Next door, the lichen-splashed dates of his neighbour's great adventure, a much older rock of ages. In the distance, looking east, the hills roll to the next ridge. It's the children's graves she finds the saddest, but then they're in Heaven now, right, if there is a Heaven. Why not? If there is a devil in a white coat in an office behind her, why not a Heaven? (But then, she wonders, what if he wasn't a devil? What if he was only a man?) For Ava, Heaven is a big, warm room with sunshine slanting through the stained-glass windows and a fully functioning typewriter with a return carriage that works. And a bottle of plonk. (Why not? It is Heaven, after all.) And Red. And a halfway decent conversation with someone who'll listen. Forget about the angels flapping about like pigeons in the town square; let's have a little dancing.

Her breath is coming back to her. Next in the hierarchy of sad things are the graves with wooden crosses already rotting in the rain, decorated by plastic flowers which are faded and brittle with exposure to the elements. Then one or two unmarked graves, cracked and hollowed, full of recent rainwater, nothing to mark them but a sunken blanket of white quartz. Couldn't even afford a stone to stop them wandering. Who weeds them? No one. No one to remember them either, she thinks, as she shall be remembered. Ava will remember. This is Ava remembering. She pats the black stone fondly, as if there's a plaster cast around a fractured limb under a blanket. There, there, better soon.

'Hello again.'

The voice startles Ava from her reverie. They've tracked her down. She spins around on her marble perch to see an old graveyard witch standing behind her. No, hardly a witch – Ava isn't superstitious, remember. She has to blink two or three times before she recognises the old woman from this morning. The woman at the fence. And hardly old either, now that Ava looks. They are about the same age, still spring chickens.

Poppy stares at Ava. Ava can just imagine what she is seeing. A strange woman dressed as a man, sitting on, sitting on – ah, Ava sees it all, sitting on her husband's gravestone. Furthermore, she can almost imagine what Poppy is thinking. Poppy almost laughs at the idea of it. Theo and anyone. Theo would run a mile if anyone even placed a friendly hand on his arm. Even his sister-in-law made him blush. Theo only had eyes for Poppy, and she for him. What a world, thinks Ava.

'What are you doing here?' Poppy asks, clutching an umbrella in one hand and a posy of flowers in the other (kangaroo paw), not a wreath.

'Well might I ask you the same question, my dear.'

'I came to visit my husband.'

She indicates the grave that Ava adorns like something from the Weimar Republic. Ava jumps up (*ouch*) and they both examine the inscription on the stone.

'Very poetic,' says Ava.

'Denise, my daughter, chose it.'

'I am so dreadfully sorry.'

'That's all right.' Poppy passes a finger under her eye. 'I don't think he would have minded.'

'No, I mean the metre is awful. Who makes up this stuff? Where's the *Miss you, old trooper*, where's the *Ride on, stranger*? It's all lambs' tails and fingerprints of the everlasting.'

'Pardon?'

'Never mind. Just thinking out loud … Only last week, you were saying.'

Belatedly, Ava notices the newness of the grave, the absence of weeds. Not even time to let the dust settle.

'Yes,' Poppy sighs. 'Very recently.'

'Again, I am sorry.'

'It's all over now. Did you know Theo?'

'Who?'

'My husband.' Poppy nods her head to the stone. 'I didn't see you at the funeral.'

'Sadly I never had that pleasure. Which isn't to say I wouldn't have enjoyed it.'

A pause to acknowledge the whole solemnity of the situation.

'Yes. This is the first time I've come here. Since the burial. It's quite lovely, isn't it?'

'Is it? I suppose so.'

They look at the grave. Ava staggers slightly.

'Poppy is my name.'

'Ava.'

They shake hands lightly, the trees swaying all around them like kelp.

'Nice to meet you, Ava … Are you feeling quite well? You seem to be hobbling.'

'I hurt my leg. But it's all right now. I was knocked down by a Sunday driver.'

'Really?'

'Truly.'

'Are you sure you're all right?'

'Fine and dandy, thanks.'

'Have you been to the hospital?'

'Don't talk to me about that place.'

'Oh. All right.'

Silence for a while, apart from the trees.

'Tell me, Poppy, did you feel the air get warmer when you came through the gate?'

'Yes, I did.'

'I think your old hubby might be partially responsible for that.'

'Do you think so? That's a nice thought.'

'It is.'

'He always used to tell me to put a jumper on.'

'Men.'

Poppy looks around at the cemetery.

'I didn't notice it before. At the funeral. How pretty it is.'

'Your mind on other things,' says Ava. 'That's understandable.'

Poppy steps forward, her own foot still slightly tender, and places her bouquet of flowers on the stone.

'He didn't care for flowers, really. I couldn't think what else to bring.'

Ava dismisses this, abruptly connecting the dots that have drifted off somewhere through the day only to return to her now.

'I see you didn't jump.'

'No,' says Poppy, recalling the morning. 'No, you talked me out of it.'

'Did I? Well, the day hasn't been a total waste, then. It's not really the right course of action, is it, Poppy, for a couple of grand dames like us to seriously consider.'

'No. What would the children say?'

'Let nature take its course. For me it's been a great day, an auspicious day, apart from being run over. Can't you feel it in the ether?'

Poppy considers this, her powdered nose to the wind: 'What?'

'Greatness.'

Ava lets the word levitate between them.

'Perhaps not the same as you. Tell me, is your husband buried here too?'

'Good God, no. I hope not,' Ava scoffs. 'I mean, I wouldn't have a clue.'

'Is he alive?'

'I've forgotten the phrase ... something French ... *à la mode* to mean I couldn't give a stuff.'

'I see. I think. And are there any children?'

Ava gives a small shrug.

'I don't feel the same way about Theo. I miss him terribly.'

'I'm sure. Did he have a beard, your Theo?'

'Just towards the end. When he couldn't shave. It was quite white. Imagine that. I'm not ready to let that image go yet. Has anyone dear to you passed away?'

It must be the grief that's making the old girl speak so forwardly. Ava looks at Poppy and there is a moment when the brimming tears in each other's eyes are of equal measure.

'Only everyone,' says Ava, then steeling herself: 'It depends in what sense you mean *passed away*.'

'Oh,' says Poppy. 'In the normal sense ... Is that what you meant by the stone foetus?'

'Who told you about that?'

'You did. This morning.'

'Yes. All dead. At least in my heart, they may as well be. And they never leave you. They sit there cold and hungry in your gut, and they roll over when you sleep, letting you know they're there, and it's your job to keep their memory alive, in the past, where they were happy.'

'So they're alive?'

Again the small shrug.

The two of them are quiet for a time, staring at Theo Whitaker's grave, and the other graves surrounding it.

'I hope Theo never leaves me. The memory of him, I mean.'

'No fear of that.'

'I must go,' says Poppy. 'I only meant to drop by some flowers and see how he was getting on. On his own. After that first night here he wouldn't have known where he was.'

'No choice but to get on with it,' says Ava. 'But please, I'll go. I'm sure you must have lots to talk about. I didn't mean to interrupt.'

'Can I give you a lift?' Poppy asks.

'What do you mean?'

'Can I drop you anywhere?'

'You mean you didn't walk?'

'No. It's too far. That's why I drove. I have a car.'

'Blow me down. No, thank you all the same, old stick. I live just over there.'

She waves her hand vaguely towards the bush at the bottom of the cemetery, where there doesn't appear to be much of anything.

'Are you sure?'

'It's not far.'

'Well, it's been very nice to see you again,' says Poppy.

'Yes, it has.'

'Perhaps our paths will cross?'

The trees wash their hands overhead.

'Perhaps ... Tell me, how long have you lived here, Poppy?'

'Here in Katoomba?'

'Where else?'

'About fifteen years. We came here after Theo retired.'

'Me too! We've both lived here in the same town all these years and yet we've never met. What are the chances? Just think of the other people in town we don't know. I'd say, on the strength of that, the odds of us meeting again are pretty slim, but nevertheless I'm a great believer in challenging the odds.'

Ava can sense she's rambling. She's driving the old woman away. Pushing her before she leaps. However, Poppy won't be driven. Instead she says:

'But Ava, after today, we do know each other.'

Ava stops talking. Did she hear that right? What a lovely thing. Someone, a living person who knows her. They touch hands again – both hands small, one of them powdered with talcum. Ava turns and lumbers downhill towards the bush track at the bottom. It's all her legs can do to stop her rolling down like a ball of dough. There are too many stories in her mind. Ava wonders what Theo would have made of the encounter. And Poppy, too, gazing after her until Ava, growing smaller and smaller, disappears into the scrub, and a Red-browed Firetail begins its high-pitched *seee.*

* * *

Past the ordered tombstones of the Anglican section towards the bush track at the bottom of the hill, a pile of grave dirt lies next to a newly dug hole with a tin lid laid over the top to keep the rain out. Ava considers the dirt as if it is somehow different from ordinary dirt. Tomorrow's entertainment for some poor chap. Keep moving, old girl, she tells herself – and to her legs: don't seize up now.

Along the track Ava at last feels she has escaped the clutches of the hospital and its henchmen. Having that place so close to the cemetery is no accident of town planning, she thinks, and further on is the town tip. Draw your own conclusions. She feels she has fooled them all, hospital staff and devil included, yet at the same time, the bush seems to be hemming her in, the trees looming over like the contemplative fingers of a malevolent creator. A child holding a bug captive in its hands, enjoying the sensation of the creature struggling to escape.

Around a bend, over the bicycle humps along the track, she encounters a dog fossicking for smells amongst the roots of some tea-tree. The dog, a blue heeler, battle scars on its snout, looks up at her, ears erect and alert. It growls. It looks like an evil thing. Ava reaches for her machete only to realise afresh that it's gone. She can picture exactly where she left it in that damned bloody buggering thieving hospital. Her best knife.

She growls back. It doesn't move. Now there's no such thing as a malevolent creator. No devil in a white coat. There is only her and this dog. Ava looks around and sees a stick by the side of the track. It's not as thick as she'd like but she picks it up. In the wilderness two living things and one stick. Their simultaneously beating hearts.

'Here, poochy; here, pooch,' she calls.

She realises that the dog is a bitch, its dugs hanging down all swollen and stretched. It must have pups somewhere.

'Where are your pups, eh? Pooch? Where are your babies?'

She talks soothingly to it, her tone contradicted somewhat by the stick. The balance tips. In an instant the dog turns and runs along the track, disappearing from sight. It must have been able to read her thoughts. It imagined the future. She is alone. The trees lean over her, creaking like bones. Lingering drops of rainwater fall from the leaves and tap on the ground. Birds here too. *Seee.* Ava limps on through the scrub and hears the bush whispering. Her leg throbs and her duodenum is aching; she's sure they've missed something there. That'll teach them, if she explodes from peritonitis of the duodenum. She uses the stick as a makeshift crutch. The dog has gone, the world's complexities reducing one element at a time. The light is gradually fading. Who is holding that lantern with its wick turned down so low? Maybe a dog holds the last gleam of light loose in its jaws, so that its drool runs down and snuffs the waning flame out. Where will she be then? For the moment it's just her and the stick. Oh, and the track.

The distance to be traversed.

She passes the soldiers' cricket oval and emerges from the bush onto the suburban streets which stretch out from the highway, these streets she knows so well, like the veins in her legs. There are no footpaths here. She passes the frames of new houses being built and older homes behind tall barricades of rhododendron and photinia, all the scenes of domestic anguish, for how could such jollity be real? The swings and roundabouts of outrageous fortune. The fine fences and fine neighbours. The house of the boy who abuses her – and here he is, playing in his front yard with a ball. No, you could hardly call it playing. Conniving. Conspiring. Perhaps this is where the dog escaped from. The boy looks up from his merciless game.

'Garn, you old nut case.'

'Eddie, get in here,' comes the other voice from behind the curtain in the window.

* * *

If only she had another life, would that be any better? How to begin comprehending the mind of another? But isn't that her job, to plumb the murky depths of another person's experience? Well, if not exactly plumb the depths, then at least scratch the surface, get under their skin like a grain of salt on a slug's tail. And if she could, how would they, therefore, see her?

It's a small town. She's not sure of the population but she may as well know everything about everybody. She may as well know what it's like to be a ten-year-old boy. She may as well know that Eddie Tebbit runs around the side of his house, immune to the cooling temperature of the air. It's a big house with wooden walls. Eddie has lived there all his life, so she may as well know everything.

She knows that Eddie must be sick of watching the witchy old bat dawdle past his fence. He'll get out of harm's way. He'll go round the back. There is a piece of rope with a stick tied to it which is tied to a tall tree. Sometimes words skip around in his mouth like marbles rattling against his teeth. He swings on his rope swing but it isn't as much fun by yourself, and after a while it makes you dizzy. There is a sandpit but he has outgrown that. There are weeds growing in it. There is his broken spade. He knows where there is a hibernating lizard.

Ava decides, yes, after his fun with the old lady Eddie Tebbit is surely bored. The mind of a ten-year-old boy is not a difficult contraption. He thinks about climbing the tree which has red sap dribbling out of it and ants eating the sap and sometimes birds eating the ants. He doesn't know what sort of a tree it is and doesn't care. From the top there is a view of the graveyard and the tip. The mind of a ten-year-old boy, thinks Ava, must be fraught with the most exquisite dilemmas. Eddie thinks about a boy called Paul Winston who has traded – traded under the threat of force – his broken watch for Eddie's favourite stone. Eddie has a bag of cats'-eyes, taws, tom-bowlers, bumbos, pee-wees and crocks of many different colours. His largest marble was his cannonball, the king of all marbles. His prized trophy. Not a word to be used in public but Eddie thinks it was *beautiful*, the veins and flaws in it that caught the light. *Was* and *caught* because Paul Winston, being older and a better player, won all of Eddie's marbles at keepsies and then, laughingly, said he would trade them back for the cannonball. He would even throw in his broken watch. Eddie, close to tears, agreed. No one understands the importance of marbles. He had no choice. Ava can imagine the intensity of the contest. Then Paul Winston promptly went and lost the cannonball while mucking around in the orchard. Eddie has thrown the watch away.

He wonders if he should follow the old witch from down the road again and spy on what she gets up to. He has probably seen her rolling rocks around outside her hut, building things. Sometimes she laughs out loud to herself. See the old witch laughing out loud. He has probably seen her hang her big white shit-catchers on the line, which is nothing but a bit of old rope strung between two trees. They are the sort of shit-catchers that witches wear. She never spots him hiding in the bushes. He is too clever; besides, he is a fast runner, so it wouldn't matter if she does, but she never does. Except that one time when she caught him setting fire to a clump of elephant grass and took his matches. And grabbed him by the ear. And when he tried to run grabbed his hair. And frightened him. Frightened him utterly. Oh, Ava remembers that.

And now he must be hungry. He flings open the back door with a bang.

'Mu-um,' he yells.

'What?' comes the reply.

'I'm hungry.'

'Have some bread and butter.'

Mrs Tebbit is in the lounge room attacking the ironing. Ava can picture the whole barren interior. Through the curtains Mrs Tebbit has seen the old woman hobble past, as she does most days. Watching Ava, Mrs Tebbit perhaps recognises her own well-trodden towpath, although her pathways are of a smaller, more ordered, more domestic nature. Or perhaps she doesn't recognise this at all. It's easier to imagine barren interiors than it is the innermost thoughts of a ten-year-old child. She has heard her son call out at Ava – *Garn* – and wishes that he wouldn't, but what can she do? Belt it out of him? Nag it out of him? He's ten. There are bigger battles.

'What's for dinner?'

'Dinner's not ready. Have you been leaving that old lady alone?'

'Yes, Mum.'

'Because I don't want you annoying her.'

'Yes, Mum.'

'I don't want you going anywhere near her.'

'No, Mum.'

He makes a sour face. But then forgets about the outside world because it is nearly time for *The Munsters* followed by *F Troop*.

Ava imagines a new scenario: Mrs Tebbit wondering if she should chase after the old lady. (That's me, thinks Ava, I'm the old lady.) Mrs Tebbit doesn't even know her name, which isn't very neighbourly. She wonders if she should catch her up, apologise for Eddie's behaviour, ask her if she's all right, she seems to be limping. Does she have enough food out there in her shack? *Why, thank you, my dear, I'm heartened by your concern.* She wonders if she should, but she doesn't. She watches the old lady go. Mr Tebbit will be home soon and he will deal with the boy.

* * *

Ah, Mr Tebbit, how many crimes have been committed in thy name? Ava realises she has no inkling as to what Mr Tebbit looks like. She scurries on, head down, wretched, trying to be invisible. There is nowhere to hide. The boy has conjured all her ghosts again. If she had her machete she'd chase him into the house, chop him up and throw him in the stew pot. How dearly she would love to chop someone up and throw them in the stew pot. She scurries past the orchard – she still has a few figs in her pocket, cut to shreds by the broken glass.

Swami Apogee, her hair up in a turban, is on her verandah, saluting the afternoon light and the going down of the sun. She waves to Ava but Ava does not stop. She cannot fabricate that story. All the tangents bouncing off her like moths off a light bulb. At the edge of the orchard, where its neat European definition blurs back into the bush, Ava steps amongst the trees. In her stealthy, trespassing way Ava loves the orchard. She wishes Angus & Robertson had bought that for her instead of the hut. The orchard reminds her of the honeyed past, when things were clear and simple, when life had a different charter, when she loved and was loved. When *the sky was aflame with possibility.* She can remember the passage exactly:

magenta clouds, iridescent, tortured, like a skin disease. Engels had (reluctantly) given us our apple money (minus compensation for a new pair of spectacles). The orchard was stripped bare, apart from a few tip-top leavings the tallest ladders couldn't reach, there for the birds. Share and share alike, we thought. The leaves of the trees hung down, looking somehow assaulted or shamed, as if they had lost a fight, or a marriage. But they would recover. Next season would be a pearler. You could tell from the formative buds lined along the branches. Our last picking money amounted to a tidy pile and we could, indeed, go anywhere. Our pockets bulged with cash. We were liberated.

'I hear they're picking oranges up Shepparton way,' I said, cogitating.

Red was tying up the strap to her swag.

'You know, Dave, I think I've done my dash with oranges.'

'Never,' I remonstrated.

'Peas. Cherries. Peaches. Beans too. The works. I've had it up to here.'

She saluted her hairline.

'Not apples?'

'Apples as well. Listen, my shoulders hurt. My fingers hurt. Look at these calluses. My back aches. My arms are scratched to blazes. I've got a rash on my collarbone here where the apple sack drags. I've had enough.'

She showed me her arms, her calluses, her rash. I wanted to kiss their aches and pains away, to soothe them back to a more sensible state of thinking about things. Think with the body, Red, not the mind. Life isn't rational. I wanted to give her the emollient of my kisses.

This is what she has tried to capture in her work. This love returns to her as she wanders between the trees, and in some trampled grass she spies a rock. It's a round rock, unusual for hereabouts, where the rocks are mostly split bits of sandstone. Ironstone too, which is said to attract the lightning during storms. (For a while Ava thought it was her.) But a round, spherical rock – a river rock, although there are no rivers up here, it's about the size of a small loaf of bread or a human noggin, speckled with mica and feldspar – lying in the orchard as if burped up out of the earth. It's as though it has signalled to her. Perhaps an old orchardist once dug it up and ever since it's lain still waiting for the next phase of its destiny. She wonders if that's too strong a phrase for it, to think of a rock as having a destiny.

Ava picks it up and carries it home, not far now. It's certainly heavier than a loaf of bread. Down to the end of the road, to the shack behind a solitary, upright telegraph pole, number 1584. Someone will treasure that number one day. It's the end of the road; beyond it, nothing but the endless flammable bush. She picks her way through the wattles just about to burst into a big breath of blossom. And here is her old bus full of treasures, patches of lichen on its yellow fenders. And here is her chimney. And here are her four fibro walls which guard her boxes of rejected manuscripts, each one four hundred pages long and typed on rose-coloured paper. Each encapsulating an aspect of her life, the romance of it, the creative force of it. Culminating in this day, this stone. Her *life*. One of the cats is waiting for her. No fresh aneurysm of feathers on the welcoming stone. She unlocks the wooden door. She goes in and tips her new discoveries onto the table. First the rock. Then, from her calico bag: the paints, the ream of paper, the sherry. Bugger, she has forgotten to get the

Weeties. She twists the cap off the second bottle and quaffs a good slug. Home. The still, quiet air within. The typewriter is grinning at her. She heaves a big, homecoming sigh. Mission accomplished.

Every moment of every day, there's your raw materials.

Beneath her boots the floorboards creak where they don't quite meet the joists. It's a sound she has grown immune to. She places the rose ream beside the typewriter and its grin broadens. All those ideas percolating in her brain, soon they'll pop like pollen: the clouds like maggots, the clay made from spittle, the threads of coincidence. She inserts her hand and pricks her finger on a sliver of broken glass nesting there with the punctured figs. She turns the pocket inside out and brushes the smaller fragments of glass onto the floor, sweeps them out the door with her straw broom. How domesticated. She hangs the coat on the back of the chair, as if someone has come to visit her. There are incisions in the pocket's cloth.

She opens the drawer in the sideboard and rummages through it. What a lot of crap she has accumulated: candle stubs, old corks, dead batteries, a gardening fork, a box of bandaids, screws, nails, pins, a withered clove of garlic with a green horn curling out of it, hairclips, cotton reels, an old pirn, a hacksaw blade, a little jar of nutmeg, stray matches, string, some beeswax, paper clips, a lifeless torch, stiffened orange peel, a knot of ginger, an egg whisk, shoelaces, paint-brushes with bristles hardened into stone, milk bottle tops, an old razor blade, a tape measure that has spewed its spool, and right at the bottom a dusty accretion of broken moths.

Plus her photos and correspondence. There are letters from Hal Porter, Douglas Stewart, Ruth Park, Miles Franklin, as well as all the others. There is an old crumpled letter, one of many, yellowing now, addressed to Oscar Wilde. She knows its insults by heart as they rise again with her bile. *A most insensitive lack of reticence in her personal affairs.* Oscar scoffs at that with withering scorn. He whom they laughed at in the dock, laughed at for loving, laughed at and locked away. She shoves the letter back. No more bullshit. She'll give them *shapeless*; she'll give them *superfluous*.

This isn't what she's looking for. She fossicks further. Here at the back of the drawer, she comes up with her tin snips, a trifle dull and rusty though perfectly functional, like a critic's acumen. She takes them outside and goes to the eviscerated shell of the old bus. She is proud of her bus, crumbs of sunlight flaking off it onto the dirt. She has tried to establish a little rockery around it, but knows it is a futile attempt to keep the bush at bay. Inside, amongst some milk urns and piles of old newspapers, she finds what's left of her roll of chicken wire. She doesn't need one of the smaller scraps scattered about the house. She peels off a length and spreads it out and cuts through the width of it with her snips. Each *click* a satisfying moment, as though she were snipping through the fingers of – who? A husband? A critic? A foul-mouthed boy? So many people she would like to take a pair of tin snips to. She knows that's not very pacific of her. The wire curls up more as each strand is cut. She even hums a little tune.

It takes a while, but eventually she has a square of chicken wire just the right size. She takes it back inside the hut and lays it on the table. The light is starting to lean across the sky. She picks up the round rock, her stone head, and sits it in the middle of the wire square. She folds up each side, cutting some incisions into the wire so they will come together neatly. They do. There is a top knot of wire at the apex, which she carefully snips off. She sutures some of the loose strands together so they hold. There. When the rock is wrapped she cuts open some brown paper bags and wraps the wired stone in that outer skin. A short piece of string tied up to hold the whole lot together like a Christmas pudding. There, get out of that straitjacket, she thinks, I did. She picks up the parcel and places it on the bread board. That will have to do. That will have to atone for the loss of her helmet and her machete. Whatever else it represents she would have trouble explaining. It's also taken her mind off her leg, which is starting to tingle.

The fire. The fire is still warm. That should have been the first thing she looked at when she came inside. What is she thinking? Without her pith helmet her thoughts are scattered all over the shop. Moths around a light bulb. She grabs a sheet of newspaper and a fistful of kindling, and quickly blows the flames to life. A practised hand. Seems like only a moment ago she was doing this. Has a whole day passed again? The flames crackle. Soon the place is toasty warm. Does she have enough wood for the night? Yes, bags. Plus there's a bucket of pine cones. She throws a few on. In a while they start spitting at her. She positions the chair holding her coat in front of the hearth, to dry the sherry out of it and, presumably, her blood. Her leg is aching mutely again, not so much from the cuts or the stitches or the tingle, but the greater thump she received from the headlight. Her femur is aching. The warmth will soon put that right. Plus she has the pills the nurse gave her. She'll need a hot-water bottle on it tonight, though. One of the rats pokes its snout out from its alcove to investigate.

'Greetings, Plutus,' says Ava. 'How goes the war?'

The rat does not reply.

Yet she knows what he's after. Ava finds the bread and saws a heel of crust off the loaf. She has to move the wrapped stone aside to make elbow room. She spreads jam on the bread and bites off a corner. How she wishes she had some hot pufftaloonies, or some rhubarb, those sweet treats from her past that she and Red used to love, to warm up her gooey innards. Her duodenum in particular. She's sure there's something wrong there. No cure. The bread and sherry will have to do. She thinks about that phrase *used to love*. That soup was nice, when was it? Was that today? Surely she's had ten meals since then. She remembers fondly a particular piece of carrot. What did they mean, malnourished? She scrapes crumbs from the bread board into her hand. She places them on the window ledge by the table along which the rats have their run. Unafraid, the two of them emerge and begin to test the air.

EVENING

Ava fetches down a sheet of cardboard from her pile of Weeties boxes on top of the tall cupboard. She lays it flat on the table, face down, and angles a look at it, the unproved vista of it, grey, what the blind might see, or perhaps her dolls if they could speak. The grain of the cardboard stretches into the distance. The shack creaks around her, the fire shifting, sticks falling on the roof, corrugated iron protesting. In the other rooms of her imagination, faint as a mosquito in the corner, she hears a new sound. She listens. Nothing. A buzzing in the brain. Her cochlea coming loose in her ear. Perhaps the corporeal manifestation of an idea being born, if that's not being, she thinks, a tad too fanciful. There it is again. Louder. It's real. The boy! She jumps up, shoves the cardboard back and goes into the bedroom, where she is able to peer out the window at the venomous world. From here she has sometimes seen menacing figures creeping through the scrub. Sometimes they throw rocks on the roof.

The shrill buzz grows louder. It's a noise she's unaccustomed to, like a cricket in a bottle, or a lawnmower falling out of the sky. Through the wattle she sees a motor scooter weaving slowly between the darkening trees. It stops. The motor cuts out. Silence and perfidy. A tall Martian steps off it. At least, it looks to Ava like a Martian. Perhaps she's imagining things. Wearing a silver space suit, with an alien's smooth helmet containing the brain and masking the hideous features. This is it, she thinks, they've tracked her down, the end has come. She's trapped. There's no back door. She wishes she had something to defend herself with. A gun, for preference. She looks around the hut. The gurlet is all she has, nestled in the wood box like a prehistoric bird.

The alien is walking towards the hut. It's a slow, measured step, working a way through the trees, as if still getting used to the force of gravity. The wattle branches flick back as the figure moves through them. Ava scampers to the kitchen and plucks the gurlet out of the wood box. Now she can hear footsteps outside, the twigs cracking. Pause. There is a knock at the door. Would an alien bother to knock? Then a muffled, alien voice calls out:

'Saviour.' Or is it: 'Favour?'

Then she realises that perhaps someone is calling her name.

The latch rises and the door gradually opens. The alien in the silver space suit fills the doorway. With a fierce battle cry Ava leaps forward, the gurlet held high in her fist, as if the ancient bird had come to life and she was seizing it by the talons. The figure jerks backwards, stumbling off the welcome stone, arms raised.

'Whoa,' the voice calls through the helmet. 'Steady on.'

160

It's not a space suit, she sees that now, just a type of motorcycle jacket. The figure quickly slips off the helmet and says:

'Hold your horses. It's me.'

Ava stares at him. The Adam's apple. It's like her heart stops. Who is imagining whom?

'Vladimir Ilyich?' The words are raw in her throat.

'Hello, Mum.'

* * *

So he comes in, this boy from the past. If not the golden past, then at least the nickel-plated one, from a time when her children were tiny and impoverished and everything was simple. A part of her has repressed the memory of nappies. The sleeplessness. That wasn't so romantic. But here they are, on a platter before her, image after image repeating through her brain. Even all the terrible things go into the soup. The fragments of that other life. What other life? This other life. See Ava fragment.

She remembers one of them eating dirt.

'How are you, Mum?'

'I'm – I'm very well, thank you.'

It's been so long since she's seen him. He's a man. Look at those shoulders. Who taught him to be a man? And is this not even more alien than she had imagined?

'Come in. Won't you come in?' she remembers to ask.

He steps inside the hut. The vision enters. She closes the door and bustles about, her mind going at a hundred miles an hour.

'Have you eaten?'

'I brought some food.'

That pulls her up short. 'Really?'

'Yes. Chops.'

They stop talking and look at one another. How long has it been since she's seen him? He was eight years old and belonged to her. He collected marbles. Is that right? Or was that someone else? Then suddenly he was fifteen and she had no claim on him. He did not know her. And there was that gap of seven years when she was locked away from the world, when her husband had her committed, and when her children grew apart from her. Out from under her shadow. Grew into strangers. Then she worked in the Auckland library and repaired the bindings of books. Her thoughts doing what they were supposed to. Then she came back to Australia, and no one remembered her. How long ago was that?

Well, they'll remember her now.

Vladimir Ilyich has his helmet under his arm, still looking a bit like a space man though without the hideous features. He smooths his hair down. She doesn't want to think of the helmet looking like a severed head. It's a helmet. It's a helmet. What if it starts talking to her?

'Don't just stand there,' says Ava, snapping out of it. 'Make yourself at home.'

Looking around the room, Vladimir Ilyich, her son, this man, places his helmet beside the bread board, where it is not dissimilar in shape to the parcelled stone. Not that he knows what's inside the parcel, nor any of the other parcels he must see scattered about the place. Does he wonder what on earth are they for? What *are* they for? She doesn't know herself. Along the windowsills and shelves the gaps between the books too are punctuated with small dolls who watch from their nooks and crannies the goings-on in the room. They'll explain to her who this stranger is. Philosophy texts are interspersed with novels and Greek drama in no particular order.

Ava watches him glancing around at the hut. It is impossible to tell what his first impressions are. He sits at the table and, after a moment, she takes the seat opposite him. It's a plain, straight-backed chair with legs that scrape painfully. The silence is awkward. A puff of smoke wafts back into the room when a gust of wind blows down the chimney. It's not drawing very well. In a corner sit the large boxes covered in a sheet containing the manuscripts, not that he knows that either, but why else has he come, thinks Ava, why else? They are the only things of value. She watches him from the corner of her eye.

He studies the old photo of his aunt as a young woman pinned to the wall, her red hair, sepia here, drifting in the breeze. She is holding a tennis racquet. One thing about Red, she was the athletic one, although she couldn't handle the picking in the end. On a cupboard where he might have expected to find cups and saucers there is a photo of a pile of paper. Human consciousness is nothing but a reflection of itself. When, in curious exploration, he casually reaches out and opens the cupboard door, he finds that the photo on the outside is exactly what is inside the cupboard. Namely, paper. On another wall a yellowed newspaper clipping showing a much younger picture of his mother, and a review of her first novel. It looks so old it might crumble if he touches it. Otherwise the decorations consist of a couple of indistinct paintings done on cardboard and pinned to an interior wall, as much to block draughts as anything else, it looks like. The primary focus of the room, he sees, is the typewriter on the table.

'What happened to your hair?'

'I cut it, Mum.'

'You used to have such lovely hair.'

Vladimir Ilyich doesn't want to pursue the topic of his hair, the floodgate that will open. To no avail. Ava wonders how she must look to him. What he must think of how she lives. Her mind, or its reflection, is rambling.

'I remember when you were little, a toddler, we had a dog, Descartes, who had to have stitches in her belly. I forget why. What ever happened to Descartes? Do you remember her?'

'No.'

'She had one of these upside-down lightshades on her neck to stop her gnawing the stitches out. It looked sad and funny at the same time. Anyway, you used to have such a sweet tooth, I gave you the big tub of honey to take over to the bench, and the dog, Descartes, saw the chance and was dancing around your feet, slavering. "Quick, hold up the tub," I cried, and you, with your eyes fixed on the dog's big pink lolloping tongue, slowly raised up the tub of honey. Raised it up, as children will, out of the dog's reach, turning it upside down – so that the honey drained down over your head, your beautiful hair, and into the cone around the dog's neck. I snatched it off you but it was too late. Inside the dog's cone the honey just about drove it spare, its tongue couldn't reach, you see, slavering about, impossible to reach. Almost went mad. You had to have your hair washed, and you cried and cried like a, well, like a kid having his hair washed, soap in your eyes and all that.'

'I don't want to hear about this.'

'I'm surprised you don't remember. Your father thought it was funny, but I bet he's not the one you think of as a tyrant.'

'I haven't come here to talk about Dad either.'

He's trying to derail her, stop her prattling. How long has she been waiting to tell this story? Or does it loop around in her head all the time?

'How long have you lived here, Mum?'

Ava, derailed, has to think. 'Fifteen years.'

'Jeez. And you like it?'

For a moment she is stuck for words, stuck at the enormity of the question and all it might imply.

'Of course. Why wouldn't I? This bed thy centre is.'

'Isn't it a bit isolated? So far from town. I had a hell of a time tracking you down.'

'It's private. Privacy, that's what I crave. A loaf of bread, a jug of wine and *moi*. My own company. As long as that old bitch over the road leaves me alone, I'm happy.'

'Who's that?'

'Swami Apogee, or whatever she calls herself. I think it's her. Someone comes creeping around here when I'm out, disturbing things.'

'What is there to disturb?'

'My *things*.'

'She's probably just checking to see if you're all right.'

'Well, I wish she wouldn't.'

'Fair enough.'

'I caught someone trying to set fire to the grass out the back.'

'Really? Who was that?'

'The boy.'

'I hope you gave him an earful.'

'I took his matches and gave him a belting. Or at least I tried to.'

'Mum, I think that was me.'

'No. It was that boy. The rude boy. No fucking respect. No brains either. He was trying to set fire to green grass in winter … Called me a nut case.'

Do these words actually come out of her mouth?

'What did you say to him?'

'I grabbed him, his arm, like this, tight, I didn't touch his hair, and I said if I saw him here again I'd peck his eyes out and eat his liver. It's what he wanted to hear.'

A pine cone pops in the fire.

'And he was suitably horrified?'

'You bet. Machiavelli's first rule of defence.'

'Mum, are you crazy?'

'That was never proved.'

'I didn't mean it like that … And you didn't touch his hair …'

'They had no evidence.'

Ava wonders if her son wonders where this conversation has come from. Where has it come from?

It's hardly the fanfare Vladimir Ilyich might have been expecting. It's like the rusty straitjackets of their roles – mother, son – must be tried on, to see if they still fit, before they can be sheared away. From Ava's point of view the house hasn't had this much conversation in it since she can't remember when. A log cracks in the heat of the fire and a healthy spark shoots out onto the floor. Vladimir quickly gets up and flicks it back into the ash with the toe of his boot.

'You'll burn the place down if you're not careful,' he says, considering the hut.

Ava stares at him, the dispenser of advice and moral wisdom. She doesn't bother to point out the old paint tin full of water for just such emergencies. She doesn't bother to point out that her terror of bushfires burning her alive, burning her manuscripts alive, keeps her very alert. What does he know? He may as well be someone she's conjured up.

'Vladimir—'

'You can call me Vlad.'

'Is that what people call you?'

'Some people call me Itchy. As in *Ilyich*. Get it?'

'Really? Vlad,' she tries it, 'why have you come here?'

'I've come to see you, Mum. Aren't I allowed to come and find my mum? And let me say, you took some finding. I've been looking all over.'

'How did you find me?'

'I asked around. How do you manage, out here on your

own? You can hardly just nip down the street if you run out of milk.'

'I walk. I'm very fit.'

Now it's her turn to want to change the subject. It's hard to find a topic that agrees with both of them.

'Will you listen to me,' she says, 'I haven't even offered you a drink. Would you like a cup of tea? Or a dollop of Penfolds?'

Vlad remembers: 'I've brought some beer.'

'Beer? Whacko. Your head's screwed on.'

'It's on the Vespa.'

He remembers his aunt telling him a schooner or two might get Ava to lay out the welcome mat. How does he remember that? Ava gives him the memory.

Her son, this man she is slightly afraid of, jumps up again, throws open the door and marches out to his motor scooter. Such energy. Ava follows him to the door, not wanting to let him out of her sight, wanting to make sure the whole thing is not an apparition. She watches him unbuckle the straps of the pannier and lift a clinking bag of bottles out. For a moment he hesitates, looking into the darkness of the pannier. Then Vlad returns and closes the door behind him. He seems real enough. He's so tall and handsome, and unlike his father, of whom Ava does not want to be reminded. How could this strapping figure of a lad have come from her? That's who he reminds her of – herself. Little old Ava. Mother and son. Her thoughts are his thoughts. How could they have taken him from her? Untimely ripped. How have the nerves that bind them maintained their link after all this time? She can feel them. Frayed at the edges, like a tooth clinging by its root, but there.

He bounces a little on his toes.

'Your floorboards feel a bit loose, Mum.'

He pulls three bottles of Resch's from the bag. King browns. You beaut, thinks Ava. They look real. Lined up on the table they look like the tines of Neptune's trident. He's about to screw up that bag and toss it on the fire when she stops him.

'No, I'll keep that.'

She takes the bag, smooths it flat, and tucks it into a drawer in the sideboard which seems to be stuffed with other paper bags. While she's there she fetches a couple of glasses and a bottle opener. No, not glasses exactly; she finds a tin cup and an old Vegemite jar. Lucky she washed the turpentine out of it. If it's all a dream then it may as well be on her terms. Vladimir Ilyich pops the cap. He pours, the froth angling up the sides. Nectar of the ancients. They clink receptacles.

'Cheers.'

'Salud.'

One thing that can be said about Ava, and she sees that Vladimir recalls it with a vague pang that pierces him: she drinks like a man. Is this what the young boy in him remembers? The amount her mouth is able to contain. Glug glug glug. She has stamina. Soon they are toasting again.

'How did you get hold of this place, Mum?'

He's making conversation. Her boy. They can talk about the weather. Rain, hail, bushfire. She supposes this is the normal thing after mother and son have been separated for such a long time, after so much water under the bridge. She wonders if she should ask him about his marble collection.

'The publishers gave it to me.'

'The publishers *gave* it to you?'

'That's what I said. Angus & Robertson. The deeds are around somewhere. It's only a hut, I'm under no illusions, but compared to how I lived before ...'

'Still, a house.'

'... Yet to me it's a temple.'

He moves around over the creaking floorboards, surreptitiously testing for termites. The dolls stare at him with their impassive glass eyes.

'Why? Why would they do that? Give you a house?'

'I ... I ...'

Ava is lost for words. She who normally has so many at her fingertips – yes – in her fingers like sparks. Perhaps it was because they, the publishers, think she deserves it: this hut. Her due. Her guerdon, for services rendered. Or perhaps, and this is a more disturbing notion, the one that keeps her salty ghost awake at midnight, perhaps they are trying to get her out of the way. What if they want to wash their hands of her? *Shapeless. Superfluous.* She did use to spend a lot of time in their offices annoying the receptionists, demanding answers to her letters. How many editors can be out to lunch at the same time? She understands about personal dynamics. Well, if that's the case she'll show them. The next novel, number thirteen, is already pullulating in her mind like a ... like a ... Words fail her. But she'll show them, all right.

'Jesus Christ, what's that?'

Vladimir Ilyich leaps to his feet and the two rats go darting back to their crevice.

'Rats,' he yelps, looking round for something to smite them with.

'It's all right. It's only Plutus and Bacchus.'

'Plutus and Bacchus?'

'Don't you have rats in New Zealand?'

He stares at her like someone at the scene of an accident, wondering if they should get involved.

'Not for pets,' he says. 'We only have possums and wetas to deal with.'

'Well, my rats are friendly.'

'They're vermin.'

'No, editors are vermin. Rats are just hungry.'

'You mean you feed them?'

'What's wrong with that?'

'They'll have your ear lobe off in the night, if you don't watch out.'

'Have you come here to berate me? After all these years. Just walk in and start berating.'

The fire crackles. Vladimir appears to force himself to calm down, making his brain think the right thing. At least, that's how Ava reads his squeamishness.

'No ... I'm sorry, Mum. It's just ... They're rats ... And ... Aren't you lonely, living out here all by yourself?'

Ava stares at him. Another impossible question.

'Oscar keeps me company,' she says.

Vlad looks around the room as if this might be the name

of another creature. One of the cats, maybe, whose presence here doesn't really seem to be paying the rent. The cats are clearly shirking their load.

'Mum,' he says, 'you're a hermit.'

All this conversation after so much silence, so long talking to her rats, and dolls, and spirits in her head. Dave, Red, Engels. Those voices are the real ones. Not this illusion of a son, a phantom from the past who can't even recall his own formative memories. Is he not real? She feels like she could put out her hand and touch him.

'I tell you what, Mum, how about I take you for a spin?'

'What do you mean?'

'A belt on the Vespa. Blow the cobwebs off. Would you like that?'

'On the motorbike?'

'Yeah. Before it gets dark.'

'I've never ridden one before.'

'You can be the passenger. I'll drive.'

She thinks about it for a split second: 'All right.'

The chances of a publisher knocking on her door at this time, after business hours, are probably quite small.

Ava drains her glass. They rise from the table and Vlad picks up his helmet.

'I don't suppose you have a helmet?' he asks.

'I did have a helmet, but I lost it.'

'It's okay, there's a spare on the bike. Better rug up, though.'

He places a wire screen in front of the fireplace, and then pulls on his motorbike jacket.

'I like your jacket,' says Ava. 'It makes you look like a space man.'

'Thanks. I like your coat. And that yellow thing.'

'It's a cravat.'

'Very nice.'

Ava wraps herself in her steaming dead bear (faux). She feels cautiously in her pocket for any lingering shards of glass. The pocket is still a bit damp but it will do. She's done a good job. They go outside. Their lungs expand with the chill of the evening air. The sun on the wane amongst the trees, but there's still bags of light. Although she doesn't tell him that the winter dusk will fade fast enough.

Vlad opens the pannier and pulls out a second open-faced helmet. He peers into the saddle bag.

'Oh yes. Here, Mum, did you lose something?'

He reaches in and lifts out her machete, sheathed in its leather scabbard.

'My knife! Where did you get this?'

She takes it in her hand, amazed.

'The hospital gave it to me.'

She takes it out and gives it a swish. Now she feels good. Now she can face the world. She unclips one of her braces and slips it through the belt loop of the sheath.

'What were you doing at the hospital?'

'Looking for you. How's your leg by the way?'

'A little scratched, but dinky-di, I think you'd say. They gave me some pills. How did you know where to look for me?'

'A cop told me.'

'A cop?'

'A young bloke. Said you'd been skittled.'

'Yes, that idiot wasn't watching where he was going.'

'He's been charged with dangerous driving.'

'Really? He said he wasn't going very fast. Skidded on the wet road.'

'You're lucky he wasn't going any faster.'

'Lucky. I suppose you're right. I'm lucky an asteroid didn't hit me. I'm the luckiest girl alive.'

'As long as you're all right now,' says Vlad. 'They were pretty cranky with you at the hospital. I'm supposed to tick you off, so consider yourself ticked. Hop on.'

Vlad kicks the motor scooter to life. Ava pulls on the spare helmet and tucks her ears into it. Giggling with excitement she hoists her leg – *ouch* – through the middle of the motor scooter. She wriggles into a comfortable position on the pillion saddle. Vlad mounts in front of her and they ease off through the wattle and the tea-tree out to the road. They bump over the culvert.

'Are you okay?'

'Chocks away,' she cries.

Vlad gives it a little throttle and they're moving, the motor labouring under the extra weight.

'Oh,' cries Ava, unused to the acceleration. And the world takes off.

As they pass the houses of the neighbours Ava takes out her machete and waves it over her head like an Araby sheik, or a Crusader charging a horse of the wild Camargue through the salt-choked marshes, hooting with delight. Mrs Tebbit watches them fly past through the net curtains, looks at her watch, lowers her head to the next chore. No, another life might not necessarily be better.

'Put that away,' Vladimir Ilyich orders, his voice muffled. 'You might hurt someone.'

'Who?'

'Me.'

She secures the knife. She remembers to hang on tight around her son's strong chest. This chest that she has given him. Returned to her like – well, it's all a bit overwhelming at the moment; the simile will come to her later.

'Faster,' she calls, but he ignores this.

They ride through the sedated township of Leura at dusk, down The Mall through the avenue of flowering cherry trees, bare-boned now, past the wealthy houses to Cliff Drive, the winding scenic snake of a road that twists and turns following the contours of the escarpment. On the first bend Vlad turns his head back to her.

'Lean into it, Ava.'

Ava does and feels like she's flying, the wind buffeting the wings of her coat like a parachute. She feels like an enormous purple lung.

'Don't let go, Mum. Hang on.'

Ava hangs on tight to her big strong salmon of a son. There's not an ounce of fat on him. She has never felt so free. It's like an old bird-dream of flying, gliding, soaring, swooping around the bends. Looking at the back of Vlad's helmet she sees someone has drawn a daisy and a little red heart. Someone loves him. A girl, or a boy, it wouldn't matter. A Russian, a Greek. As long as there is love to melt a stony heart. She wonders what sort of a person would love her son? They ride around the cliff tops past the Bridal Veil Falls – she must go and look at them one day – past a lonely paddock with a lone sheep grazing, the road curling like a girl's hair ribbon. They ride past the houses with the million-dollar views to Echo Point. What – here already? – here at the spot by the fence where she spoke to that poor woman. When was that? Was that just today? And then at the cemetery, yes: Poppy. Look at me now, she'd like to call, look at me now. They fly up the great hill of Katoomba Street past the scenes of Ava's diverse adventures. Here is the hole in the road now guarded by barricades and winking orange safety lights. Here the church. Here the post office. Here the café. She wonders if Angus & Robertson have received her manuscript yet? How long will it take them to reply this time? How long that endurance test? And here the recent scene of her accident. She looks for her topi in the gutter where it rolled but there is nothing there but a bit of rubbish. The roads are now dry. The shops all closed. They ride on. She is amazed how quickly she is able to revisit her day, these places that on pony shanks took her so long to accomplish. It's like her life in fast motion, flashing before her eyes. Please don't let it finish in the hospital, she thinks. Perhaps she will get a Vespa for herself. Maybe Douglas Stewart will stump up the credit? An advance. She'll give him an IOU while they argue over *The Saunteress*. She'll have some riding lessons. She'll go on a road trip. Maybe to Springwood to visit her good friend Norman – Norman Lindsay, if you please. Imagine how much more time she would have for writing if everything was this easy, if she didn't have to walk everywhere. Shopping would be a doddle. How liberated she would be if time could be made this obedient.

Once past all the shops they ride up Bathurst Road, where it looks like someone has been chopping down trees along the railway line. They turn out to the highway, where Vlad really opens the high-pitched throttle. Wasp of the open road, she thinks. They travel adjacent to a west-bound train, the lights in the windows revealing an illuminated chain of carriages, passengers reading, sleeping, simply staring out at the twilight, flickering like Zeno chasing his own tail. The scooter begins to pull ahead and Ava smacks her thigh (*ouch*) as if she is riding Gala Supreme in the Melbourne Cup. The train hoots. Ha! She lays her head against Vladimir's back. Even through the helmet she can feel the vibrations of the tyres on the road, the beating of her son's heart with its indecipherable code.

In a few minutes – only a few minutes! – they arrive at Medlow Bath, the next town in the string of villages stretching over the mountains. How has she ended up here, after all these years? What coalition of fates has brought her to this point in her life? Again it's too big a question. More immediately what has brought her here is Pegasus in the form of a whining, flatulent motor scooter. And look, here is the Hydro Majestic Hotel with its famous domed roof like a Spanish onion. Vladimir Ilyich parks the Vespa, kicks out the stand, and they dismount. It's so long since she's been here. Has she ever been here? She must have, because it's clear as a dream.

'Better leave the knife, Mum.'

'What?'

'Take the helmet off.'

'I can't hear you.'

Vlad takes his own helmet off and Ava copies him.

'Better leave the knife here.'

'Oh … Not on your life, sonny boy,' Ava hoots, exhilarated with the air in her face, the adrenaline powering through her. The wind has made her eyes water with glee.

She goes over to the side of the road, where a long line of agapanthus has been planted to form a border between the footpath and the hotel grounds. With a few practised swings Ava lops off some of the dried, left-over flower heads.

'Take-that-you-pedants,' she pants.

'Calm down, Mum. They're not going to let you in, waving that around.'

Ava stops. 'We're going in?'

'Sure. Why not?'

She sheathes the machete and transfers it from her braces to the pannier of the scooter. She wonders if she should brush her hair, but then she hasn't brought a brush. Vlad doesn't seem too worried about that. The great onion dome of the main building, called CASINO, rises over them in the dusk, glowing green with verdigris. From a certain angle it looks Russian Orthodox, but only for a second. Ava imagines the Cossacks flying through the air overhead. Vlad offers his arm and together they walk up the gravel drive to the double doors and the vestibule. She is glad he is walking slowly for her, not that she has any trouble with the act of walking; her wound is quietly swaddled and the painkillers are humming nicely. They take time to admire the garden, the crenels in the high walls, the exotic architecture of the buildings. The pinnacle of civilisation. This might be a moment of truth: her boy looking after his mother. It might be the garden of Gethsemane.

They enter the hotel with its famed ballroom (where Melba allegedly sang), the inner dome of which rises up to the high arched roof. Ava gives a little warble, but no, the acoustics are dampened from the day's rain, and Melba was a different kettle of fish altogether, bossing people about. Let Melba write a prize-winning novel and win a medal for it, if she can.

'Not bad, eh, Mum,' says Vladimir Ilyich. 'The only comfortable place in Australia, they say.'

'The acoustics would have helped,' replies his mother, this strange little woman beside him. She looks at herself through his eyes, daydreaming she is Melba. Vlad considers her face upraised like a crocus to the vast dome. They'd have told him this would happen – his aunt, his sister – that he would never understand his mother. Ava imagines that he dearly wants to understand her, to at least have made the effort of trying to understand her. And yet, like many sons, the last thing he appears to want is for her to understand him. That would be too intimate. It would allow her to have opinions about his life that might have to be listened to. His own private failings he would like to keep to himself. Paralysed by ambivalence – she knows how that feels. He does not want people getting too close, and is comfortable with fostering a mutual sense of distance. This is how we have evolved. Look what this amoeba has become.

It's been near a quarter of a century since he last laid eyes on his mother. It doesn't bear thinking about too closely. He is the one on guard. He won't welcome her in. He is the hermit.

They move beyond the ballroom, past the reception desk through to the Belgravia lounge, swept along by the line and flow of the building, rubbing elbows with chaises longues, lush sofas and armchairs deep enough to sink in. These are scattered about the room like geometric chess problems, lit by subtle reading lamps and chandeliers, little pockets for a range of private tête-à-têtes. Ava's so excited she would like to bounce and jump on every seat, like a monkey with an itchy arse.

A few gentlemen reclining in the deep armchairs are smoking cigars, their fireflies glowing in the inner dusk. In fact a maid – is that a maid? – is going around turning on the first lights. An energetic porter carries someone's suitcases upstairs. Ava would like to smoke a cigar. Vladimir Ilyich (why did she call him Vladimir Ilyich again?) ushers her out of temptation's way, up a long claret-coloured passage called Cats Alley. Elegant standard lamps burn in corners, their peach shades softly glowing, the empty settees waiting for the next passersby to perch on them a while. Ava remembers she was so desperately sick with Vladimir before he was born, so stricken with ceaseless nausea, she was going to call him Toxin. It sounded like a proper name. Lucky she didn't go down that road. Imagine the questions at the schoolyard gates.

She dawdles up the carpeted corridor so she can examine, in some amazement, the series of incongruously violent images adorning the walls painted by – can you make out that scrawl? – by Arnold Zimmerman. Look at them! Roman centurions skewering lions with bloody spears. Gladiators lopping the heads off Christians. Muscular, giant charging goats – now there's a charging goat! Wild-eyed horses rearing at the claws of pouncing leopards. Black panthers snarling on the backs of terrified, badly painted bovine creatures. Other animal contests – bears and tigers, dragons and knights – all rather grisly for a relaxing family health resort, especially if it was called the only comfortable place in Australia, but Vlad's mother is taken with them. At least Ava imagines her son seeing his mother taken with them. All that armour. Those weapons. The marble ruins of antiquity. Spears and pikes and sabres and, in the background, some lovely desert and jungle scenery. Perhaps she only wants him to think she is taken with them.

At the end of the 'alley' in the bar and dining room there are large windows looking out over the valley. It's not yet dark. The last of the sunlight casting the valley in a dry, lemony haze. The paddocks all golden below with the bush creeping into it like a blanket falling off a bed. The orange cliffs catch the light and hold it, but for Ava the busy spectacle barely rates a second look.

'I think I fancy an absinthe,' she declares. 'That's what Oscar would have in a place like this.'

'I don't know if you'll get that here, Mum.'

'What about a cigar?'

'I didn't know you smoked cigars.'

'I don't. But I have a sudden urge, and one thing I have learned is to give in to your sudden urges.'

'Even if they're illegal?'

'Cigars aren't illegal.'

'Fair enough. What do you think of the view?'

Ava glances at the scene: 'As Oscar said: *A really well-made buttonhole is the only link between Art and Nature.*'

'Yes, well,' says Vladimir, irritated, 'I suppose to you that makes sense.'

'To me and Oscar ... I tried to procure some morphine today, but was prevented only through lack of supply.'

'What do you want morphine for?'

'A sudden urge.'

'But why?'

'To dream. To yield to my dreams.'

He stares at her. They find a table by the window. Vladimir gazes out at the spectacle, perhaps finding he cannot look at his mother. A waitress brings them a menu.

Seeing it he gulps. Such prices. And, counting, there are nine courses. Not dishes, courses!

'Just drinks, thanks,' says Vlad, playing the part.

Studying her menu, Ava asks: 'What's in a Screaming Lizard?'

'The ingredients are listed on the back, madam.'

Ava says, 'I just want to hear you say them.'

'Oh. Crème de menthe, green chartreuse and soda water.'

'Ah, chartreuse. Lovely. Yes. Bring me two.'

The girl glances at Vlad.

'I'll have water, thanks,' he says.

The waitress looks confused.

'Is that two for you, madam?'

'Of course. And would you have a cigar?'

'I'm afraid there is no smoking in the dining area.'

'It's all right, I don't smoke. Tell me, is Conan Doyle here? Did a little bird tell me that?'

Vladimir comes to the waitress's aid. In another incarnation she could have been the sort of girl he'd have liked to ask out, and might have – the cliché strikes – taken home to meet his mother.

'Mum, Conan Doyle is long dead.'

'But he ate here, didn't he? I seem to recall. Or did I make that up?'

'I think he did,' says the waitress, who may as well be called Verity. 'It's in the pamphlet.'

'Did he order a Screaming Lizard?'

'I don't know … I'll see if I can find out,' says the poor girl now called Verity.

'Mum,' sighs Vlad, 'she's just trying to do her job.'

'What? It's a legitimate question.'

There is a pained silence between them while they wait for the drinks. Other people are eating their entrees, talking amongst themselves. Whispering in her ear Oscar has another point to make about the view: '*When I look at a map and see what an ugly country Australia is, I feel I want to go there and see if it cannot be changed into a more beautiful form.* That has been the ultimate purpose behind all my work too.'

'I see,' says Vlad.

They proceed to debate the merits of the view and views in general. Good points and bad. This one's too Turneresque for Ava's liking, as if Zeus's beard had caught fire in a field of opalescent, corrugated wavelets. Whew! Sometimes she exhausts even herself. Vlad doesn't ask her to repeat it. *Stylistic excess*, that's a phrase she doesn't want to hear again. When the drinks arrive, green as algae in an unlilied pond, they clink glasses.

'To you, Mum.'

Ava says, *'Alcoholidays.'*

Vlad does not smile. It's galling. They sip.

'So cruel, so royal a drink,' she says, her hand assisting with a regal wave.

Sometimes she makes no sense. Sometimes she's sharp as a tack.

Not much more can be said about the view, as the windows continue their darkening. Ava skates her gaze about the opulent features of the room, the curlicues in the cornices, the brass door handles, the ornate rococo frames about the mirrors.

'Nice carpet,' she says.

Vlad looks at the carpet and has nothing further to add. The ice tinkles in his water glass. Their conversation seems to come out of thin air.

'I've been wondering,' she says, 'how you've coped with a name like Vladimir Ilyich.'

'I've had a long time to get used to it.'

'You haven't found it to be a burden?'

'What doesn't kill me makes me stronger.'

'I suppose so. Who said that?'

'I forget. Anyway, at least I didn't run off and get another one when it didn't suit me.'

There is still a little spark between them. *You will eat your porridge. I will not.*

Is this why's he's come? Revenge for his name? The soap in his eyes.

'Well, since you bring it up, I've never had the chance to ask you as an adult, but why did you give me that name?'

'Oh, I don't know. A rush of blood to the head.'

'Great. Named after a rush of blood.'

'I must have been come over with a fit of patriotism.'

'But you're not Russian.'

'No, but I have the blood of the Cossacks coursing through my veins.'

'Really?' Vladimir drinks. He must wish it was vodka.

'So I thought at the time. Change it if you don't like it. My name,' says Ava, 'has been a great – counterpoise – to me.'

They drink. Ava swirls the green pond water around in her mouth. She puts down one empty glass and begins on the next.

'I worked for a while as a book repairer in the Auckland library,' she reminisces. 'I don't think I knew you then.'

He doesn't know what to say to this because he clearly remembers when he was fifteen going into the library to catch a glimpse of her in some dimly lit back room, head down in meticulous work over a damaged book. It was soon after her release from the mental institution. His mother, from whom he crept away. And did she look up and see him? And is this not her memory?

After a while Vladimir speaks: 'Okay, Mum, now it's my turn. Seeing how you live, I've been wanting to ask you about your health. The hospital said you absconded.'

'Which hospital? Auckland?'

'No. Here.'

'Oh … My health? Dear boy, thank you for your concern but I'm as fit as an oyster.'

She pounds her chest, straight away wishing she hadn't. When she stops coughing she says:

'How long have you wanted to ask me that?'

'Oh, that's … that doesn't … Is your leg okay?'

'Nothing another Screaming Lizard won't fix.'

'Mum, I'm being serious. I was wondering about your – the state of your—'

'You mean my mind?'

'Well. Yes. Your mental health.'

'You're very presumptuous, my son. I told you before. Nothing was proved. I did not pull that boy's hair.'

'What? No, not that. Mum, I'm talking generally, Auntie Red told me, it's common knowledge.'

'What is? Rubbish. Anyway it's a bit late in the day to worry about that, isn't it? You never cared last time. You didn't even visit when I was in that awful place.'

'Dad wouldn't let us,' the son protests, and she can hear the buried whine in his voice. 'Dad said you abandoned us. He said you were – dangerous … There was that time we were in that rowboat and it began to sink and you jumped overboard—'

'*I* didn't jump overboard. *He* jumped overboard. I hugged you to me.'

'My memory isn't very clear. It was so long ago. And we were only kids. We were scared.'

'And that's supposed to be a source of comfort to me, is it?'

'Mum. I'm sorry. I didn't come here to fight with you.'

Ava looks as though she wouldn't mind a fight with someone. Seven years she waited for someone to visit, tell her what was going on. Seven years. Vlad drinks his water. As the waitress approaches he gives her a surreptitious shake of the head and she diverts her course to calmer waters. Ava sneers. All this pussy-footing around the fairy floss of her nerves.

Gradually Ava's resolve fades. The muscles in her jaw let go and her cheeks hang limply off their bones. There's no one worth fighting. It's an old battle she's lost many times before. Night after night, why must she revisit the infinitely varied scenes of her failure? Why has he brought her to this point of dejection, perfectly formed in the pit of her gut? She feels suddenly tired. She feels her age. Her leg is giving her gyp. The painkillers wearing off.

'I think I'd like to go home.'

'Are you sure? I thought I'd bring you up here for a treat. Get you out of that house. My shout!'

'Two Screaming Lizards is more of a treat than I've had in many a moon.'

'Okay, if that's what you want.'

'It's all been a bit of a shock. The accident, and seeing you again.'

'I'm sure. A shock for me too.'

'What do you mean?'

'Nothing.'

Ava upends her second cocktail.

'Bottoms up,' she says, but her heart isn't in it. For a moment her lips are green. Drinks like a man.

Vlad picks up his helmet and goes to the bar to pay the bill while Ava pulls on her smelly coat. The golden cravat limp at her collar. Unbelievable how much those two drinks have cost. He pockets the change, Ava pockets the coasters, while the waitress called Verity watches them go: a funny couple she has forgotten as soon as the door swings shut. Who on earth was Conan Doyle?

* * *

It is dark at last outside. Severed foliage litters the path beside the scooter. The ride back is weirdly a sober affair. She's frightened of falling off. Ava hangs on tight and buries her face once more against Vladimir Ilyich's back. This stranger. This amoeba. What if she pulled out her machete and sliced his throat like Medea? No, that probably wouldn't help, and she'd definitely fall off. Her leg is throbbing rhythmically. She remembers to lean into the corners. The passing cars seem fast and dangerous, dreamy, their headlights like asteroids, all on their mysterious orbit. Or collision course. Her zoetrope flickering past. Her arms hug her grown son, and while there is some ill-defined memory, a spark of warmth in this human contact, the wind whips around her, inside her coat and out, and she is cold.

NIGHT

THEY RETURN TO THE HUT, and even at night Ava, something breaking in her, sees how bleak and forlorn it is, how it must look to the eyes of another. Stupid old bus in the headlight, perched up on brick pylons like a fish caught in a net. The colour of the shack indistinguishable from the surrounding dun-coloured scrub. Grey grey grey. The jagged sheets of asbestos lying about the place in the grass. It looks to her newly opened eye somehow diminished. Her teeth chatter and the damp pocket of her coat is cold against her thigh.

Wattle saplings brush against them as Vlad weaves between the trees and switches off the ignition. The Vespa's engine ticks in the newborn stillness. He remembers to give her the machete. It's such a shame about the topi, she thinks, but maybe someone handed it in to the police. Maybe, lost and bedraggled, it might wend its own way home. The breeze hisses softly in the tree tops. She sees, through his eyes, the fact that the hut has only one door. There's hardly room for two. If there had been two there might not have been enough room for the inside. The hut would simply have been a brief passageway, an interruption, no more than an interlude between one part of the outside and another. And they, phantoms, passing through.

Inside, Ava remembers that to stoke the fire is the first thing which needs her attention. She turns her face to the ash. Vlad, making himself home in the kitchen, unwraps his chops and slaps them into a fry pan battered as an old hubcap. He shifts the strange parcel wrapped in brown paper off the bread board. It's surprisingly heavy. He places it next to another on the sideboard.

'What is all this crap, Mum?'

'Posterity.'

Parcels of stones and feathers and chicken wire. In one of them, she can't remember which one, there is an orange tuft of Eddie Tebbit's hair. Vlad shrugs. Ava sees that her son doesn't understand. Why should he?

She pours the beer.

'Do you have a sharp knife?'

She has only one sharp knife.

Using the machete he dices up some potatoes. Once the fire's blazing, things are much more cheery. What was she worried about? It's just her old dolour doing its rounds. The smells, the sizzling fat and its fabulous smoke. There is a man, a living man in her house, at the stove, cooking up a storm just for her. When did that last happen? Did it ever happen? Her son. Look at his broad back. A man. Out of the ether.

She sets the table, first moving the typewriter aside. Where shall she put it? Here on the draining board next to the sink? No, it might get wet. There's no room, so cluttered is the place with posterity. She picks up the machine holus-bolus and takes it into the cold bedroom. She thinks about a few homey touches, a tablecloth might be nice, but remembers there isn't one. She used it as a curtain to keep the light out a couple of summers ago, and now it's nothing but a faded dishrag. Instead she snaps open the packaging and takes two pink foolscap pages from the new ream and lays them on the table as place mats. It's a special occasion after all.

The spuds bubble away in their pot, steam fogging up the kitchen window. Vladimir has found candles in a drawer full of miscellaneous gubbins, that's the only word for it, and has placed them strategically about the room. Hang the expense. *More candles*, she reminds herself to put it on the list for tomorrow. While the potatoes boil, Ava takes off her boots and a sock to examine her foot. She scratches at a rash between her toes. Vladimir sees how pale and tiny it is. The long, yellow nails. The thin bones within. His mother's foot, fragile and almost translucent. Hard to credit the work it's done over the years. She puts the sock back on. He sees that her socks are different colours.

Remember, thinks Ava, their evening, this refined pleasure is finite. Oscar will need to direct the conversation before she is overcome. In a while Vladimir drains the spuds, splashes in some milk, some salt and butter, and mashes them up with a fork. He serves up the chops onto two china plates of different size. There aren't any others. He places them on the table.

'Have you got any sauce?' he asks.

'Sauce? Do you know I forgot to go to the shops.'

'You went to the shops today.'

'Yes, but I forgot my list.' Then, as if remembering, 'And I got knocked down by a lunatic driver.'

'You were lucky.'

She studies him seriously, the wrinkles beginning in his cheeks, the eyebrows about to go wild with age. They're real, aren't they?

'Do you know,' she says, 'I think I was run over today by a figment of my own imagination.'

'Maybe you were.'

'Though it felt real enough.'

They sit in candlelight opposite each other. There's plenty more mashed potatoes in the pot. Silence while they eat. The clinking of cutlery. The sipping of their beer.

'I wish you'd get rid of those rats.'

'Well, that's not logical,' Ava snorts, offering no further elaboration.

Vladimir places his knife and fork together and eases back, stretches his spine against the backrest of the chair. After licking her fingers Ava leans towards him and says:

'Can I have your bone?'

'Sure,' he says lightly, but cannot bring himself to look at her sucking it.

After their meal Vlad boils the kettle and makes a pot of tea. Ah, the endless cups of tea, Ava rhapsodises. He doesn't twirl the pot six times and so it won't taste as nice, but it's nice enough. She stirs in some sugar, watching the tiny maelstrom. *Whirlpool*, that's the word she was thinking of before. Even her words are leaving her. Vladimir drinks his tea quickly then rises to wash the dishes at the sink.

'Let me help you.'

'No, Mum. You rest.'

However, Ava does not know how to rest. Rest eludes her. In the corner of his eye she's hobbling about, getting under his feet. Making sure he's doing it correctly. It's her house. Her spirit seems to pace relentlessly. What would she be doing if he wasn't here? What does she do every night?

She watches his back as he passes the clean dishes from the sink to the rusty dish rack. He does not want her to help him, to lay claim to him. It's not an act of union, of bondage, it's just a chore. It doesn't take long.

'What about these spuds, Mum?'

'Leave them. I might have them for supper.'

While he works his mother hums to herself in her pacing. It takes a little while to recognise the tune. Then – she's humming: *All things bright and beautiful, all creatures great and small*, and this somehow fills the air with melancholy horror. When he's finished he turns to her and says:

'I read that book you wrote, Mum.'

She's astonished. 'Which one?'

'The one about the apple pickers. Dave and Red. What was it called?'

'*The Apple Pickers.*'

'Yeah. That's it. Dave, that was really you, wasn't it, disguised as a bloke.'

'Oh, all that happened before you were born. Red and I had the time of our lives.'

'It was good, Mum. I enjoyed it.'

The fire spits and chuckles to itself. There is a crack in the mortar between two bricks of the chimney where a little dribble of smoke seeps out, gathering at the highest corner of the roof.

'Thank you, Vladimir. That's nice to hear.'

'Call me Itchy.'

'Itchy.'

'Bit late coming, I know, but, yeah, I got a laugh out of it.'

'Charmed, I'm sure.'

'So if you were Dave, and Red was Auntie Red, who was Engels?'

'Engels was your father. Engels was' – she almost sings – 'every man who done treated me wrong.'

'Well, you certainly taught him a lesson.'

'Who, your father?'

'No, Engels.'

'Yes, I did, didn't I … Have you seen her, your aunt?'

'I see her occasionally. Christmas, and so on. She lives in Wellington now. She's worried about you too.'

'I'm so busy I rarely have time to think of her.'

'I find that hard to believe. There's a photo of her just there on the wall.'

They consider the photo of Ava's sister, Red, her heart-shaped face, and the absence with which it fills the room.

'Does she still play tennis?'

'Not for a long time.'

He finds a tea towel, pretty threadbare, and turns back to the dishes. Keeping busy.

'Leave them,' she says.

So now there is nothing but the awkward adieus, painful, mixed with ambiguous relief. They are at the door, moving outside into the night. The air is icy. The drizzle has stopped, on again, off again, but is mounting its forces, getting its wind like a boxer between rounds. Vladimir stuffs the spare helmet into the side pannier as if he is trying to drown a brown dog. He kicks the Vespa out of gear and wheels it to the road. All dark everywhere. The stars extinguished. Ava trails along behind. Vladimir pops the bike on the stand then turns back to his mother. This small old woman who knows so little and yet who knows so much more than him. It's not a knowledge he cares to own.

'Good night, Mum.'

'Goodbye, son,' she says. 'Itchy, I like that.'

'It's because I had nits at school.'

'Oh, I see. Much more prosaic. Perhaps you might drop by for some breakfast in the morning? I know where to get some eggs.'

'Sure, Mum. That sounds like a good plan.'

However, she knows he won't come. She knows that if she got up early and went to Gearins to intercept him he'd be gone. He's doing what sons do.

She sees it all, parading before her in some lost vision. There is no resolution. He leans down and gives his mother a kiss. She is his mother; he can't deny that. People kiss their mothers. She feels almost coy. He kisses her, and for a moment she clings to him, kisses him on the mouth. Then he breaks away and pulls on his silver helmet so she can't get at him anymore. He slips on his jacket. Swings his leg through the scooter and stamps on the kick-starter. It belches into life. The headlight illuminates the nearby trees, the overbearing foliage. He gives it a rev, and then pulls slowly into the road, bumping over the ditch. These final moments sear themselves into her eyes. Then the tail light slowly dissolves up the road past the orchard, getting smaller until it turns the corner and is gone.

Ava is on her own with the silence, the moon failing to break through the shreds of the canvas sky.

She stares after the vanished motor scooter. It's not coming back. She realises she's alone, outside, like a rabbit out of its burrow with all the night's eyes alert to her. There is not even the light from a single window to interrupt the darkness. Apart from her own. It's freezing. She limps back. The fire roars for a moment in the draught as she opens the door. In the ensuing silence it's like the great human bulk of him is still present in the room. The echo of his presence. The shadow of his energy dancing with her. She does a private little jig. But her elation does not last long. Already she feels it, the spirit of his presence, dispersing like mist.

She slams the door shut behind her. Then opens it and slams it shut again with more power, just so as to have the satisfaction of slamming it properly. It doesn't quite make the noise she's after. The candle flames flutter wildly. She cannot think of the best words to accompany this gesture. Perhaps *fuck* might be one. A raw scream another. They will come to her later, no doubt. After the event.

So she stokes up the fire and soon the house is cooking.

Little claws scratching up in the ceiling where it is warmest. It's almost too hot, but she's reluctant to open the door again to let any of the heat escape. The windows she can't open. They've been stuck for years. A sheet of cardboard is taped over one broken six-inch pane. The eye she has painted on it stares at her. The rats are sitting on the table, waiting. Her house. Better than anything she had in New Zealand. Ava, here, alone as she ever was. Why didn't she just hammer him with the gurlet? She is so glad he did not remind her of his father, although the timbre of his voice had a ghost in it. Perhaps that was the point of his visit, to make her confront her ghosts. Perhaps in it there was a message from Red. Well, to confront things, there is only one way that she knows.

She goes into the bedroom and is momentarily surprised by the incongruous image of the typewriter resting askew on her pillow. No rest for the wicked. She picks it up and its heavy indentation lies square on the pillow. She lugs it out to the table and places it down. She has an idea for the next chapter of *The Saunteress*. Hang on, that one's already gone, posted this morning. A living, breathing, haunted thing. Soon to be in a bookshop near *you*. What now? All right then, she has an idea for something, and part of the poem she lost in the pub this morning returns to her. She plucks two sheets from the new rose ream and inserts them with a skilled hand.

My one and only heart-shaped leaf
I would never find another
that would bring me similar relief
from who I am and who I am not.

She shrinks into the maimed sunset
beyond the shadowed seas
a halo of pure light encir.ling her,
the s.n hanging its tired o.d head at l.st
in th. w.st, th. fu.l m..n ca.ght in th. tr..s
tr.pp.d like a .ish in a ne.

She'll attend to the corrigenda later. Doesn't quite sound like the beginning of something, she thinks, the setting sun and that, but something she can build towards. A fish in a net, where did that come from? She peers closely at the last few lines. She can still make them out, even though the keys have punctured the paper like Braille. She can feel the dots under her fingers. One of these days she's going to have to buy a new ribbon.

Ava pushes the typewriter away. She doesn't feel like writing tonight, which is not like her. Normally the muse would have her up half the night, and then struggling for sleep. It must be the shock. The accident has petrified her blood. There's still a bottle of Resch's left, so that'll put the icing on the cake. And the sherry. Her kidneys are aching gently. Perhaps in her dreams her son, or her sister, will tuck her in so she might sleep at last. The night is pressing in. Two books. Do two books stand up against the weight of the night? The weight of the silence bearing down on her? Are two books enough? Is that all the noise she has in her soul? Of course not, but it seems they will have to do. The impermeable darkness punctured and punctuated by those two fading stars, the light by which her life shone brightest. They will have to whisper for her. Almost extinguished now. Outside the night is blind, hissing with the susurrant ebb and flow of the tree tops. Her little inner spark tossed on the waters.

She scrunches up the pink foolscap placemats and throws them in the fire. The chop fat makes them catch and blaze quickly. Then, from the pile atop the cupboard she picks the next sheet of King Willy Weeties cardboard, cut from the box she flattened this morning. There are no more Weeties, she remembers, she'll have to get some tomorrow. And a ribbon. Maybe she should make a list. The throbbing in her leg is starting to get worse. Those stupid nurses, they should have fixed it properly. She labours to her feet and finds the painkillers the hospital gave her. There are four left. She takes two and swigs them down with a mouthful of beer. Then she takes the other two.

She spreads the cardboard out on the table. She fetches her paints and brushes from the old turpentine jar on top of the bookshelf. The books all in place, leaning like soldiers at ease. The dolls sitting like sentries or gargoyles between them. Where did she put her paints? The new ones she bought today. Ah, yes, she remembers, on the bed. She finds the parcel and tips it up. She has quite a collection now, quite a palette. There is the Armanth Red, the Artichoke, the Bangladesh Green, the Cadmium Yellow, Orange and Red, the Dark Byzantium, Electric Lime, Worn Leather Shoes, Tweed Coat. It's as much about the names as the colours. She could move through the alphabet – no, the spectrum of colours, hovering like a rainbow over an apple green field, naming each one until she gets to … potato grey, congealing in the pot on the bench like a sort of cement, a sort of melted brain. A portrait of her coagulant, midnight soul. Maybe tomorrow she'll wrap that up in wire and brown paper.

But she's not there yet. She changes out of her good trousers. Wouldn't do to get paint on them. Changes into her pyjama pants. She unscrews a few lids and squeezes paint onto a saucer (a clean one). She takes a deep breath. All these things in a life to take account of. All the raw materials: a fingernail, a cramp, a woman at a fence. The fence itself. A hole in the side of the road. A grave. A Screaming Lizard. Her headstone on the bread board. A tuft of ginger hair. And is it her life, or someone else's? She takes a brush and dips it into a fanciful colour called Flattery. She starts at twelve o'clock and, moving anti-clockwise, her wrist traces a circle to the left. Of course the paint runs out so she dips again and, starting at midday, or is it midnight? traces to the right until her two arcs have joined to form a perfect line. Not a circle. The line is perfect, just what she was hoping to achieve, not the circle, but the line, which might be a river stone inside a cage, or it might be a silver space helmet, a face uplifted to the sun, or the sun itself gazing down. It might be anything. A heart-shaped leaf swollen to its extremities. She does not know what she has begun, only that it feels like the most important thing she has ever attempted. And it's not finished. That's the beauty of it. It never ends. She stands up and stares at it. Her line. Coming back to itself. Complete and hollow both. She looks at the black windows. She can see her own reflection looking back from the glass, an old woman, hair awry, all her fervour gone. If only she had another life, would she want it? Is that Ava or someone else? By some other name. It's getting late. She'll finish it tomorrow. What now? What now? Once more it's starting to rain. The mildew on the ceiling will like that. And who's that lying prone on the floor? See Ava lying prone. See, she's only got on one slipper.

AUTHOR'S NOTE

Ava Langdon is a thinly disguised fictional version of the Australian writer Eve Langley, sadly neglected these days. I first became interested in her when researching a play about a fabricated meeting between Langley and Eleanor Dark, in their time two relatively well-known writers who never, as far as I can establish, met. Yet this is not a historical novel. It couldn't be. Little is known, or documented, about Langley's last days or months or even years, as her mental health deteriorated in her hut in the Blue Mountains. When I first saw it the hut was still standing, surrounded by the strange wire parcels that she made. Now it is a sad, dilapidated ruin. Over time she became increasingly reclusive. It is not even certain exactly when she died. If anything she was probably more addled than I have portrayed here. Anything I have presumed could therefore only be fiction; there is no evidence that she did any of the things I have suggested. As such, this is not a biographical novel. I have used a few biographical 'facts' and aspects of Langley's personality, recordings of her speaking and, of course, her writing, to inform an approximation of her voice, a voice which still has resonance for me. Any words or actions I have given to Ava can only exist in the realm of the imaginary.

Quotations from Oscar Wilde come from:
Redman, A (ed.), *The Wit and Humour of Oscar Wilde*, Dover Publications, New York, 1959.

Other books I have found useful include:
Frost, L (ed.), *Wilde Eve*, Random House, Sydney, 1999.
Thwaite, JL, *The Importance of Being Eve Langley*, Angus & Robertson, Sydney, 1989.

ACKNOWLEDGEMENTS

A number of people have read various drafts of the manuscript and given generously of their time and expertise. I would like to thank Deb Westbury, Carol Major, Alice Major and Philip Dodd for reading earlier versions of *Ava* at different stages of her evolution and making very helpful comments. Also Annie Byron and Maureen Green, who helped me to hear the formative cadences of Ava's voice. I would also like to thank my agent, Gaby Naher, for her faith in the character and in me. At UQP I would like to thank Madonna Duffy and Ian See for their brilliance and enthusiasm, as well as the marvellous eye and ear of my editor, Judith Lukin-Amundsen. Last, but not least, my family Barb, Liv and Eamon. Thank you.

More fiction from UQP

A LOVING, FAITHFUL ANIMAL
Josephine Rowe

It is New Year's Eve, 1990, and Ru's father, Jack, has disappeared in the wake of a savage incident. A Vietnam War veteran, he has long been an erratic presence at home, where Ru's allegiances are divided amongst those she loves. Her sister, Lani, seeks to escape the claustrophobia of small-town life, while their mother, Evelyn, takes refuge in a more vibrant past. And then there's Les, Jack's inscrutable brother, whose loyalties are also torn.

A Loving, Faithful Animal is an incandescent portrait of one family searching for what may yet be redeemable from the ruins of war. Tender, brutal, and heart-stopping in its beauty, this is a hypnotic novel by one of Australia's brightest talents.

'Utterly compelling … This is a striking and highly original novel for readers of Australian literary fiction.'

Books+Publishing

'*A Loving, Faithful Animal* is a novel of startling imagery and power. A beautiful and, at times, shocking exploration of the fault lines that run through families and of the far-reaching – and occasionally devastating – consequences of decisions made by those who govern us.'

Chris Womersley, author of *Bereft* and *Cairo*

'A remarkable work of fiction. Deft, lyrical and deeply moving.'

Wayne Macauley, author of *Demons* and *The Cook*

ISBN 978 0 7022 5396 6

NAPOLEON'S ROADS
David Brooks

What are the crimes of love, anyway, but fragments of passion broken from their moorings, evidence of a kind of shipwreck? (But what kind of ship? Where was it? What was its name?) Or crows, a flock of them, high in the air, fighting against a wind that no-one can see.

David Brooks' mastery of the written word is both evocative and compelling in this, his fourth collection of stories and his first in almost twenty years. These pieces capture unforgettable images of streetscapes and heartscapes, grappling with concepts of time and memory, tenderness, mortality, creativity and solitude.

Profound and illuminating, *Napoleon's Roads* is a celebration of the rich possibility of language and expression from one of the finest poets and prose stylists in contemporary Australian literature.

'The reader … is likely to be engrossed from the start by the bright intelligence and muted sensuality of the latest performance by one of Australia's most skilled, unusual and versatile writers.'
The Age / The Sydney Morning Herald

'Being at the intersection of text and life, theory and poetry, I would have said these stories form the best instance of Australian postmodernism I have encountered to date, if they weren't also suffused with humanity.'
Aashish Kaul, author of *A Dream of Horses*

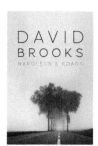

ISBN 978 0 7022 5391 1

THE ASH BURNER
Kári Gíslason

Growing up with his father in a small coastal town, all Ted knows about his mother is that she died when he was a boy. His father has brought them halfway across the world to start anew, but her absence defines and haunts their lives.

When Ted meets Anthony and Claire, an intense friendship begins, carrying them to Sydney and university. They introduce him to poetry and art, and he feels a sense of belonging at last. But as the trio's friendship deepens over the years, Ted must learn to negotiate the boundaries of love, and come to terms with a legacy of secrets and silence.

Written with extraordinary grace and sensitivity, *The Ash Burner* explores beauty and desire, grief and loss, and the search for one's true self.

'At once contemplative and precise, *The Ash Burner* is an exquisitely written novel that left me deeply moved by its tender exploration of beauty and grief.'

Hannah Kent, author of *Burial Rites*

'This is a beautifully written novel … Its characters are vivid, its landscapes evocative, and its narrative given shape and power by the revelation at the end.'

The Age/ The Sydney Morning Herald

'A thoughtful work that should leave an impression long after it's been put down.'

Readings Monthly

ISBN 978 0 7022 5342 3

Lightning Source UK Ltd.
Milton Keynes UK
UKOW06f0325270617
304104UK00013B/934/P

9 780702 254154